A Mail Order Bride For Wyatt

The Carson Brothers of Kansas
Book Three

By Carré White

This is a work of fiction. Names, characters, places, and incidents either are the product of the author's imagination or are used fictitiously, and any resemblance to any persons, living or dead, business establishments, events, or locales is entirely coincidental.

A MAIL ORDER BRIDE FOR WYATT

Published by Love Lust Story
Copyright © 2014 by Carré White
Cover art by Erin Dameron-Hill
ISBN: 1495362264
ISBN-13: 978-1495362262

First Print Edition: February 2014

Books by Carré White

The Carson Brothers of Kansas

A Mail Order Bride for Charlie
A Mail Order Bride for Bronson
A Mail Order Bride for Wyatt
A Mail Order Bride for Grant

The Colorado Brides Series

An Unexpected Widow
An Unexpected Bride
An Unexpected Annulment
An Unexpected Mother
An Unexpected Love

The Arizona Brides Series

An Audacious Spitfire

Sonoran Nights

CONTENTS

One

San Antonio, Texas, July 1871

I had been up since five in the morning, wanting to finish the piles of laundry that had been delivered yesterday, so I would have the afternoon to myself. Mrs. Holden strode towards me in the hallway, and I loathed that I would have to speak to her.

"You're not done already, are you, Eugenia?"

"Yes, I am. I finished five basketfuls this morning. I've done my work for the day."

Her lips turned down. "Then you should've done Sofia's share. Where's she been anyways? I haven't seen her for two days."

Sofia, my roommate, had not been feeling well. "She's ill, Mrs. Holden. I'm checking on her shortly."

"If I'd known you were this lazy, I never would've hired you."

That statement was entirely unfair. "I've been at work since dawn. I've done my baskets. Everything is clean, dry, and folded."

"I hired you to work all day. There's plenty more to do where that came from."

I wished more than anything that I had not encountered her in the hallway, hating the condescending way she glared down her nose at me. I had done my job! "Marta and Liz have their own washing. I'd be chastised for taking someone else's work. Sofia will have to manage her duties when she feels better. You're more than welcome to come check on her. She's had a fever for two days." The welfare of her employees wasn't something she was concerned with in the least, as I had often labored under illness. Sofia's condition worried me, though. I had never seen someone so unwell. "She might need a doctor."

"I doubt that. You girls are as lazy as they come."

Anger, white-hot and unreasonable, coursed through me, but I held it in check. "I've finished for the day. My baskets are empty. Everything's neat and tidy."

"Then you should take in more work."

I did not want to have this discussion a moment longer. "Excuse me, Mrs. Holden. I've somewhere to be."

"I doubt that," she muttered. "Lazy as your

good-for-nothing mother."

The urge to scratch her eyes out had me seething. I brushed past her, knowing that if I said another word I would lose my job. Not only that, but she owned the boarding house and she would surely throw me into the street. Hurrying towards the stairs, I clambered up several flights, until reaching the top floor. The sounds of a baby crying and someone shouting echoed down the hallway, while the smell of tobacco lingered. Opening the door to our room, stale air greeted me. It was dark, as the curtains were drawn, but Sofia's form was beneath a blanket.

"Are you awake?" She mumbled something in reply, and I hurried to open a window, wanting fresh air, although it would be hot and humid. I glanced out at Commerce Street, glimpsing a line of freight wagons pulled by teams of oxen. These arrived and departed every day. The stench was at times almost unbearable. "I can't leave it open for long." I turned to face the bed, wondering how Sofia could sleep in this heat under the heavy blankets. "How are you?" I felt her forehead, which was hot to the touch. "Oh, no." Pouring water from a pitcher, I held a cup to her mouth. "You should drink." She did not reply, leaving me with a sense of dread. "I'm gettin' a doctor."

"No, I'm…fine," was her feeble response. "I'll be better tomorrow."

"The fever should've broken by now."

"It's stubborn."

"You're stubborn."

Sofia was due to travel soon, as she had agreed to be a mail order bride. She had been communicating with a wealthy cattle baron, who lived in Kansas. I doubted if she would be well enough to join the cattle drive north, which would be an ordeal all its own.

"I'll…try to drink now." She struggled to sit, her long, tangled hair falling around her shoulders. Grimacing, she gasped.

"What?"

"My leg hurts."

She had stepped on a nail several days ago, and she had been in pain ever since. "I should look at it."

"I'm fine."

I held the cup to her mouth, yet she struggled to drink. "You need some broth. You're far too weak."

"I'm just not that hungry." After a few sips, she collapsed to the bed. "Are you free for the day?"

"I am."

"I'm sorry I'm such a pest."

"You're not a pest."

I sat on the bed, moving hair away from her face. Sofia and I had been living together for eight months now. I had known her most of my life. My family was unorthodox, consisting of the women I knew in the local brothel, because my mother had been a soiled dove. She had serviced the men of the cattle trade and cowboys, among others. Sofia and I had vowed not to succumb to this lifestyle, but it had been difficult to resist. Working as a laundress was hard, tedious labor, and the pay was low. If I sold myself, I could earn in a day what it would take an entire month of laundering to make. But I had obstinately refused to seriously entertain this notion. Sofia had found a way out. She had secured her future by agreeing to marry a stranger.

"You should read to me."

I knew what she meant. The letters that Isaac Hardin had sent were vastly entertaining, as his writing style was flamboyant, but the handwriting was atrocious. He was considerably older than Sofia, a man in his late forties, but he had survived two wives, both of whom had not provided him with children. In need of an heir, he had taken matters into his own hands and published an ad in the newspaper. All Sofia spoke about these days was her new life in Kansas and how she could not wait to be the wife of a cattle baron.

"I could read them again, if you want."

"He sounds like a lovely man."

A lovely, old man. "I suppose."

"I know you disapprove." Her voice was barely

above a whisper.

"I don't disapprove, but maybe I'm jealous. You'll experience an adventure most women only dream about. I envy you. I'll be here washin' and ruining my hands, while you drive north with a passel of cowboys."

"There are dangers."

"In everything, I know." I felt her forehead again. "Are you still so cold?"

"Yes."

When the fever broke, as it had several times over the last few days, she had felt clammy and her skin had dripped with perspiration. But then it would flare again, and she would shiver in bed. "I should look at your leg."

"If you want."

Lifting the blankets, I grasped the bottom of her nightgown, pulling the garment up. She had hurt her right foot, having stepped on a nail, which had jutted from an old staircase in the basement. The initial injury had been small, a round puncture wound, and now, there were deep purple streaks running beneath the surface of her skin.

"Gracious." This could not be good. "We need help, Sofia. It shouldn't look like this."

"What does it look like?"

"Purple rivers taking over your leg. It's past your knee now."

"I see."

"Nothing's gotten better."

"Then go get help. Mr. Hardin sent some money. I'll have enough to pay a doctor."

"I really should." A sense of urgency propelled me to my feet. Grasping a bonnet, I flung it over my head, tying the sash beneath my chin. "I'll be back as soon as I can."

"All right." She didn't seem to have the energy to lift her head.

"I won't be a few minutes." Hastening from the room, I ran down the hallway to the stairs, finding several women loitering, smoking.

"How's Sofia?" asked a short, stout woman. "Haven't seen her in days."

"She's dreadfully sick. I'm off to get Doc Winston."

"Is there anything we can do?" asked Matilda.

"I…I don't know. I can't talk now."

"Good luck, honey," drawled Loretta, whose accent was the thickest of them all.

"Thank you."

"Give a holler, if you need anything," said Matilda.

Reaching the next landing, I called, "I will."

I had known Doctor Winston for years. He had come to the aid of the working girls, whenever there was sickness or unwanted pregnancies. He was respected and trusted. My mother had been fond of him, although he had not been able to save her when she had fallen ill. She had trouble breathing from time to time, her wheezing often keeping her up at night, but that last attack had been fatal, and there was nothing anyone could do.

Hurrying down Commerce Street, past the street vendors and blacksmiths, I slipped into the doctor's front door, finding his secretary behind a desk, while several people waited to see him.

"I need the doctor. It's an emergency."

"It always is," she intoned.

"Please, Mrs. Bender. It's my roommate. There's something wrong with her leg."

"Have a seat. I'll see when he's available."

"Thank you."

She returned a moment later. "He'll be out in a moment."

I glanced at those waiting, and none of them seemed as ill as Sofia. When the doctor appeared, wearing a pair of rounded spectacles, I got to my feet. "I need help, sir. Sofia's not well. She's been feverish for days, and her leg has purple streaks on it."

His gaze drifted over me. "Did she have an accident?"

"She stepped on a nail, sir."

His expression darkened. "I see."

"Can you help her?"

He glanced around the waiting room. "Anyone gonna die in the next hour if I'm not here?"

"I have a broken arm, sir," said a man in a wide-brimmed hat. "But, I can wait."

"All right. This shouldn't take long. Hold down the fort, Mrs. Bender. I gotta make a house call."

"Yes, Doctor."

Relief nearly overwhelmed me. If anyone could save Sofia, it was Doctor Winston.

Two

The boys and I were on our way to San Antonio to pick up a thousand head of cattle, all of which would be driven to Abilene, Kansas. I had been working this run for two years, after having given up thieving and cattle rustling, knowing that career would see me dead and buried far before my time. My only vice nowadays was liquor and women, both of which I planned to indulge in and often. Drinking was discouraged on the drive, which meant I had less than a week to get my fill. I knew better than to squander a single moment being sober.

"Give me another, Pat."

"Yes, sir." He poured amber fluid into my glass, not spilling a single drop.

"Thank you."

"You in town for long?"

I passed through Sequin often, stopping at Marvel Saloon coming and going, unless I was on a drive. "Just a night. I'm headin' for San Antonio."

"I see. You're still workin' the Chisholm Trail?"

"Yeah, but probably not for much longer."

"You finally found a pretty lady to settle with?"

I gave him a look. "Uh, nah."

He laughed, "That's right. You're not the settlin' kind."

"Oh, I am, cause I don't plan to be on the road forever, but I'm keepin' my options open. I've got this last drive, and then I'm gonna see my family. Two of my brothers just got married, and the youngest had a baby girl just recently. My ma's been bringin' in mail order brides."

"What?"

"It's a long story." I chuckled to myself, thinking how Charlie and Bronson had fallen victim to the marriage curse.

"Oh, lordy. You don't say. Mail order brides? She's an enterprisin' woman."

"That she is."

I grinned, as a memory registered. My mother was a force to be reckoned with, having raised four unruly boys after pa's death. He had lost his life in a skirmish, fighting a band of Missourians before the war. My brother, Bronson and I had gone east shortly after, fighting for the union, although we both hated the experience. I had been wounded at Bristoe Station in Virginia. The scar on my back was a constant reminder of my service to God and country and the long, cold nights on the battlefield. My history had made me a bit of an outcast amongst those I rode with, as many of them were Confederate sympathizers, so I kept this bit of information to myself.

"Mothers always know best."

"Not this time." Movement in the doorway held my attention, as one of my boys approached. "Hey, Nelson."

"I thought this was where you'd be."

I held up a glass, nodding. "All week, son." I tossed the contents down my throat. "Yes, sir."

"Shep got here this mornin'. I was in San Antonio. I was gonna wait for you there, but somethin' came up."

"Great." I could care less about any issue at the moment, as I was officially off-duty.

"I have a telegraph from Hardin. We got more than cattle to transport."

Unconcerned, I waved to Pat to pour another splash of whiskey into the glass. "Uh-huh."

"Did you know he's been romancin' some woman from San Antonio?"

"That old coot? Nah."

"Apparently, she's a mail order bride or some such nonsense."

Pat overheard that bit. "We were just talkin' about them catalogue women, weren't we, Wyatt?"

"Yes, we were. Two of my brothers fell victim to their charms." This notion was so ridiculous; I began to laugh.

Nelson removed his hat, running fingers through unruly hair. "Well, I'm glad you find this funny. We're supposed to take her with us to Kansas. How you like 'em apples? You laughing now, boss?"

My face fell. "What?"

"We gotta drag her sorry butt all the way to Abilene."

I sat a little straighter. "A woman on a cattle run?"

"It appears so."

This thought was so disagreeable; I got to my feet, adjusting my belt, while glaring at Nelson. "I gotta hit the privy. When I come back, we're gonna start this conversation all over again, but, this time, I don't want to hear about no woman joinin' the drive, you catch my drift?"

He shrugged. "Suit yourself. I'm just passin' the word. This Sofia person is coming along, whether you like it or not. It's the boss' orders."

Disgusted and thoroughly rankled, I brushed by him, heading for the back door. It wasn't until I returned, that some of the anger had begun to lessen. Sliding onto the bar stool, I reached for the glass. Nelson had ordered whiskey as well. "I'm gonna need to see that telegraph."

"Yes, sir." He pulled out a wrinkled piece of paper. "Here it is."

"Thank you." I took the paper, glancing at the printed words.

Wyatt Carson San Antonio Texas July 6, 1871

Arrange for transportation of Sofia Parker Room 36 Fielding Boarding House Commerce Street San Antonio Texas to Abilene Kansas any means necessary

Isaac Hardin Abilene Kansas

I struggled to make sense of what I had just read. "Any means necessary? If she dies, I guess we just toss her over a horse and trot her in?" A fit of laughter produced a belly laugh that left me coughing. "Oh, that's rich."

Nelson shook his head. "I can't believe you're laughin'. We're gonna be stuck with this woman for two months! I'd rather stab my eyes out with a fork than have to deal with a female passenger. What in tarnation is she gonna do with herself?"

"We'll use her for coyote bait. That'll keep 'em from the animals."

Pat, who stacked bottles, began to laugh. "Oh, that'll do it too."

Holding his head in his hands, Nelson seemed beat. "God help us," he muttered.

"Is this for real?" I squinted, looking at the paper. "You didn't print this to get my goat, did you? You're pullin' my leg, right?"

"I wish I was."

A female would not only be a burden but an unnecessary distraction for the twenty-odd men I employed for such drives. I re-read the telegraph, squinting at the tiny script. The words remained the same no matter how many times I went over them. Irritated, I got to my feet, tossing a few coins onto the bar. "Well, this night's not gettin' any better. I'm gonna mosey to a parlour house for a spell. See you in the mornin', Nelson."

"Yes, boss, bright and early."

I strolled from the saloon, which reeked of stale booze and chewing tobacco, as spittoons had been placed around the room. I had quit that habit a few years back, preferring to have an occasional cigarette instead, but I seldom indulged in them, as I was saving every penny. I hit the boardwalk with a purpose, feeling a familiar itch that was in need of a thorough scratching, and only a pretty scarlet lady would do the trick.

Most towns had several brothels, which offered up enough of a variety for a man's amusement. Reaching my destination, I pushed open the door of the Cherry Factory, inhaling the heavy scent of perfume. The interior was darkly lit, with the lamps turned down low. Several men loitered in the parlor, presumably waiting to be called up.

"What can I do for you, mister?" asked a short, plump belle.

"A drink would be a start," I drawled. I wasn't in the habit of rushing through an establishment such as this, wanting to savor the experience, drinking and watching, until a woman caught my eye.

"Yes, sir." She sashayed towards the other side of the room, where two girls stood, dressed in nothing more than silk robes. When she returned, she handed me the glass. "I'll open a tab, if you want or will you pay per drink?"

"The tab's fine." I took a sip, relishing the heady taste of uncut whiskey. What I drank at the bar wasn't nearly as smooth, and it tended to give me a bellyache in the morning.

A woman sauntered across the parlor in a frilly, short skirt and bodice, which brimmed with cleavage. She sat at the piano, plucking the keys. I relaxed against the red velvet sofa, eyeing the room, while men smoked and talked. One got to his feet, ascending the stairs with a woman. The anticipation of the evening was just as pleasurable as what occurred in the rooms, and, with this in mind, I sipped the drink and let my worries drift away.

"Is there a song in particular you want to hear, sir?" asked the woman at the piano.

"Not really. That was nice."

She smiled. "Thank you."

Two men descended the stairs, placing their hats on their heads, while striding towards the doors. An older woman in heavy face paint appeared, her sharp gaze missing nothing. She made a beeline for me. "I don't believe we've met." She held out a gloved hand, which I shook.

"Wyatt." My last name wasn't necessary.

"Are you looking for anything in particular, Wyatt?"

"I'll know it when I see it."

"I have several new girls brought in from back east just this morning."

"I imagine." She was the madam of this establishment.

"Will you hire for the hour or the night?"

"Depends on the girl."

She sat next to me, leaning in, while her bosom heaved over the corset. "I see." There was a certain glimmer in her eye. "You may have two at once, if you can't decide on just one."

I laughed, "You sure know how to sweeten the pot, honey."

She purred seductively, her eyes flashing. "Oh, do I ever. For a handsome man such as yourself, I'm liable to throw the second girl in for free."

My eyebrows lifted. "Now you've got my attention."

Her hand was on my thigh, rubbing gently. "I

can assure you, Wyatt, that you won't soon forget the pleasures you'll experience here at the Cherry Factory."

"I gotta say, the name itself speaks volumes."

"If these walls could talk…"

"The whole town would bleed from its ears."

She threw back her head, laughing, while two girls approached. I eyed them, finding the blonde appealing, as she smiled shyly. I always did prefer the less ostentatious ones, although the idea of two at once…was compelling.

Three

Yet two days later, Sofia's condition worsened, as she slipped into unconsciousness. Doctor Winston had bled her repeatedly over the last forty-eight hours, but even the leeches would not save her now. The marks on her legs worsened, as an infection of the blood took over, ravaging the young woman. I sat teary-eyed by her bedside, often holding her hand, while she quickly lost the battle to live.

When I had failed to appear at work, Mrs. Holden had fired me, paying the wages she owed. I was told that I would have to leave the boarding house. With Sofia nearly gone, I had begun to pack my things, although a plan had emerged in the process, as my instincts for self-preservation took over.

The sad, desperate hours of the early morning

left me with the burden of loss and the thought that life was far too short. My mother had died before her thirty-fifth birthday, and now Sofia was gone. I did not need to feel her pulse to know that she had passed. Those pale features and sunken eyes were enough evidence, and I dared not venture any closer.

I sat for ages across the room staring at her. "Poor Sofia," I whispered. "May God embrace you in his loving arms. May you find peace. I'm so sorry I wasn't able to help you." I grieved for as long as I dared, knowing my time was at hand.

I had read the letters that Isaac Hardin had sent her, finding his handwriting difficult to understand. Someone slid a telegraph under the door, which I knew was for Sofia. She was to meet a man by the name of Wyatt Carson in the lobby of the boarding house early in the morning, but I would not be able to stay here another night. Twinges of shame registered, because the plan I had concocted was to assume her life. I had little choice now. It was due time I struck out to find greener pastures and leave San Antonio behind. There was nothing left for me here other than memories now and even those should be forgotten because most were unhappy.

Sofia and I were nearly the same size, and I packed only the best dresses, leaving the tattered calicos behind. The thought of joining a cattle drive was strangely exciting, mostly because I had always had a bit of a wild, adventurous streak. I was ready to break free. I was eager for the unknown.

Without telling anyone of Sofia's passing, I slipped from the room that evening, clasping a heavy bag in one hand and a key in the other. I would leave it on the stairs, not wanting to stop at the front desk. I intended to spend the night at a hotel and return in the morning to meet Wyatt Carson. The lodgings in question were across the street and down the boardwalk, barely two minutes on foot. Once I had secured a room, I deposited my things on a chair, finding the space sparse, yet comfortable. I washed as best as I could, using a pitcher and bowl, dunking a cloth repeatedly. Once I had changed into my night things, I slid beneath the covers, but sleep was difficult to achieve, as I tossed and turned.

Sometime in the night, a commotion outside caught my attention, and I flung the covers back. There were screams in the street and male shouts. I hastened to the window to watch, realizing that someone had found Sofia. Mrs. Holden was aware that she had been gravely ill, yet she had not bothered to visit once, nor had she offered any help. She would have to deal with the body, and, for that, I felt a deep guilt, but none of this was my fault or my responsibility. I had left it all behind.

"Good bye, Sofia," I murmured. "I love you, girl."

A wagon appeared, as men hastened into the building. Moments later, they brought out a body covered in a blanket. "That belongs to me!" shouted Mrs. Holden. "You can't take the bedspread!"

Disgusted by the spectacle, I slammed the window shut, returning to bed. It would be another hour before I slept, tossing and turning and feeling dreadful about the situation. In the morning, after I had dressed, I worked my long, dark hair, winding it into a bun at the nap of my neck. Catching sight of myself in the mirror above the dresser, a woman with pale skin and dark eyes greeted me. My mother was of Mexican heritage, although I was told her father had been a white man. Her expressive eyes and rare beauty had been helpful in her career, because men found these desirable—exotic. I often watched her apply kohl to her lashes and rouge to her cheekbones.

She had dusted powder over my nose more than once saying, "Someday you'll do this, my dear. Then men will stampede a path to your door, *mi tesoro*. They'll lay roses and diamonds at your feet."

Not wanting the same career, I had done what I could to earn a living, finding odd jobs, while struggling to afford room and board. If assuming Sofia's identity would lead to a rich husband, although he was reportedly old, I was quite eager to meet him. I dreamed of a better life. My hands alone bespoke of the many hours I had spent washing clothing, the skin dry and cracked from abrasive soap. It would be a luxury to have soft, smooth hands and lovely long nails.

Setting these thoughts aside, I hastened to pack my things, tossing what I owned into a leather bag. I tied the sash of the bonnet beneath my chin, while a sense of anticipation raced through me. If all went well today, I would embark on an adventure that would change everything. I left the room a moment later, hastening to the boarding house, where, upon my arrival, the entryway was empty. I took a seat waiting for Wyatt Carson, while praying no one observed me. I had worn one of Sofia's dresses, a lovely gray and white skirt with a fitted bodice. It was the smartest piece of clothing I could find, hoping to make the right sort of impression. Tapping my booted foot, I waited in silence, as people came and went.

"Oh, Lord!" gasped a voice.

I glanced up to find Marta staring at me. "What?"

"I thought you were Sofia for a moment. Isn't that her dress?"

"I can't say."

"You know she passed last night, don't you?" Her look grew suspicious. "You steal her things?

Those need to go to her next of kin."

"She has no one, Marta."

Her hands went to her hips. "Some friend you are." Her voice had risen. "You sneak out in the night and take what doesn't belong to you. You tell no one Sofia died. You should be ashamed—"

Panic drove me to my feet, needing to flee. She had every reason to censure me, but it would ruin the plan I had hatched. "Goodbye!" I rushed out the door and straight into a man, who felt as hard as a wood plank. "Oh!"

"Whoa!"

My bag fell from my hands, toppling down the steps, while a passerby glanced in our direction. "Tar balls!"

The man I had collided with bent to retrieve the bag, handing it to me. "You got rocks in there?" His smile creased the edges of his eyes.

"No, sir."

"Tar balls, huh? Never heard that one before."

I had not gotten a good look at him, until then, seeing someone with a pleasantly weathered face and clear blue eyes. His grin caught me by surprise, as a thunderbolt of tingles erupted in my belly. I had never been courted before, nor had I ever been kissed, but, as I stared at his full, pink lips, I wondered what they would feel like pressed to my own.

Before I could chastise myself for such

wayward thoughts, he murmured, "They sure make 'em prettier every day."

"Pardon?"

"Sorry. I'm supposed to meet someone. You got your bag, right?"

"Yes, sir. Are you Wyatt Carson?"

He blinked. "Yeah."

I held out my hand. "I'm Eu-Sofia Parker, but…um…I do prefer to go by my middle name of Eugenia."

"You don't say." While digesting this information, his eyes drifted over my face. To my astonishment, he grimaced, placing his hands on his hips. He stared across the street, uttering, "Blasted heck!"

"Sir? Is something wrong?"

"This whole situation is wrong. A woman has no business being on a cattle drive, especially a pretty one. Like I don't have enough things to worry about," he muttered. "Now I gotta worry about you."

"I'm sorry, sir." Glancing over my shoulder, I spied Mrs. Holden and Marta approaching. I grasped his arm. "We should go!" I dragged him down the steps. "Where's your wagon?"

"Over there." He pointed to a nearby conveyance.

I rushed to it, tossing the bag in the boot and hoisting myself onto the seat. "We really should go now. Right this minute!"

He seemed perplexed by my haste, but once determined to move, he joined me, taking hold of the reins. "Is everything all right?" His eyes were shaded beneath a wide-brimmed hat.

"Yes." I glanced over my shoulder. "Oh, go!"

"Eugenia Madsen! I beg a word with you." Mrs. Holden approached.

"GO!"

Wyatt Carson called to the horse, the animal trotting forward, while Mrs. Holden and Marta followed. "You have some explaining to do, young lady!"

"Go faster!"

He glanced over his shoulder. "Is there somethin' I should know about?"

"Nope."

"Why are those women following you?"

"I've no idea."

"Who's Eugenia Madsen?"

"They must…be mistaken."

He chuckled, "All right." The horse sprang forward increasing the distance, while Mrs. Holden and Marta gave chase, but we outpaced them by several lengths.

I sighed with relief.

"You wanna tell me what that was about?"

I glanced at him, admiring his handsome profile. His shorn beard gave him a manly, rugged look. I wasn't going to answer that question. "Are you taking me to Mr. Harding?"

A brow lifted. "You mean Hardin, don't you?"

Oh, goodness. "Y-yes, of course."

"That's what I'm supposed to do. I'm meetin' my boys on the outskirts of town." He glanced at my attire. "You got anything older to wear? We're gonna be on the trail for about two months, honey."

"Two months? That's quite a long time."

He nodded. "Cattle average about fifteen miles a day, cause they gotta graze. Otherwise they lose too much weight and they won't be worth nothin'."

"I only have these types of dresses."

"I guess they'll do then. You know how to ride a horse?"

"Not especially. Is that a requirement?"

He rolled his eyes. "Oh, lordy."

"I'm sure I can learn, sir, if it's important."

"Everyone has a job, including you. Looks like you'll commandeer the chuckwagon."

How hard could that be? "I can do that."

A line of freight wagons had entered town, and, as we passed them, I gazed at the place I had called home for the last eighteen years, knowing that I would never return. Instead of feeling sadness at this circumstance, a sense of elation swept through me. This was my opportunity to start over. I had a new dress, a new name, and would soon have a rich husband, who would take care of me, beautifully. Nothing this exciting had ever happened to me before, and I was determined to enjoy every moment.

What was even more fascinating was Wyatt Carson, who sat straight in the seat, grasping the reins, while his features remained equable. He wore denim trousers and a pale blue tow shirt with a brown vest. He had brought a jacket, but it hung over the seat. It was humid. The sweltering heat of summer was upon us, and it would only worsen as the day wore on. A thick leather belt encircled his narrow waist, with a gun holstered at the side.

"You're gonna wear a hole through me, if you keep starin' like that."

For having just met him and not knowing a thing about his character, I sensed his goodness, as I felt instantly at ease. "Two months?"

His head swiveled in my direction. "What?"

"We're on the road for two months?"

"Yeah."

Most women would be horrified to be at the mercy of the elements for that long in the company of rough-looking men. Their manners would more than likely be lacking as well. For some reason, the thought of being in this man's presence left me oddly contented. There were worse things than traveling with fine-looking cowboys.

Sensing my attention, he muttered, "You gotta quit starin' at me like that."

Hardly chastised, I asked, "Why?"

"I ain't on the menu."

What on earth did *that* mean? "Come again?"

"Oh, never mind." His jaw had hardened, as he mumbled something under his breath.

Four

I cursed up a storm in my mind, using words I never dared utter out loud. Having been sent on a fool's errand, I had retrieved Sofia Parker from the Fielding Boarding House, but I had been unpleasantly stunned by her appearance. Flawless skin, a full, inviting mouth, and dark, almond-shaped eyes had filled my vision. A man could get lost in those eyes, which would lead to certain disaster, no doubt. Stories of the sirens who bewitched sailors, leading them to their deaths, came to mind or Mark Antony, who, because of his obsession with Cleopatra, had died in disgrace. Miss Sofia Parker was dangerous. No doubt about that.

My boys waited on the outskirts of town, having gathered a thousand head of cattle for transport. The drive would be tedious and exhausting, yet the prospect of having to endure two months with a beautiful woman was nearly intolerable. I'd had more than my fair share of amusements in my lifetime, more harlots than you could shake a stick at, but none of those ladies could compare to the innocent beauty of this woman's face. Her eyes were the color of rich, dark wood surrounded by the thickest, blackest lashes I had ever seen. She looked like a porcelain doll, with delicate cheekbones and a rosebud mouth that was made for kissing.

Blasted! I had to stop thinking about that!

She was staring at me again…which I felt acutely. Every nerve ending in my body was on high alert; my senses were naturally attuned to the interests of the female sex, as a predator might pick up the scent of a wounded animal. I had her attention, which was a disaster. Her inexperience shone through as well, but, instead of repelling me, it was like a beacon daring me to investigate. All of this boded ill, as she was the fiancé of the man who had hired me to bring cattle north.

I had finally settled into a profession that was on the right side of the law for once, having given up thieving and rustling, wanting to be a better man. The years after the war were difficult, my soul having been rattled by the things I had seen and done. I had finally come to terms with it all, even the nightmares that plagued me had diminished, and now this. How was I going to manage two months in the presence of this woman?

Although the ride was short, the damage had been done, because I was wound up tighter than a spool of yarn, my neck aching with strain, while I struggled to focus on the task at hand. It didn't help that Eugenia smiled at me prettily whenever I swung my head in her direction. Blasted girl!

"There are so many." She gazed at the sea of cows; all of them had their heads bent, grazing.

"Yes, ma'am."

"Have you known Mr. Harding long?"

"Hardin, and yes. I've worked a couple of his drives."

"Where are you from?"

"Massachusetts originally, but my family moved to Kansas when I was a teenager."

"Is your family still there?"

"My ma and brothers are."

"And they farm?"

"And raise cattle."

"I see. I've never been anywhere but San Antonio before."

She seemed contemplative, staring at the animals, which now were on every side and closing in. Dust up ahead was from one of my boys, who had spurred his horse to a gallop. I was responsible for a dozen men, who had brought five to ten horses apiece, with a horse wrangler to manage them all. A cook by the name of Marty oversaw the meals, while the lovely Miss Eugenia would travel with him, although I had yet to inform him of the good news. The wagon we were in would carry the bedrolls and other essentials, along with the meager belongings of the cowboys, mostly a change of clothing or two.

My traveling companion seemed enthralled, her eyes the size of saucers, as she took in the scene around her. A bonnet protected her skin from the sun, the straw concoction simple, yet fine, with a black satin bow tied beneath the chin. I cursed myself for staring at her again, irritated that she was so lovely. I would have to watch her carefully around the men, but, since spirits weren't allowed on the trail, I hoped they would not cause too much trouble.

As we approached the chuckwagon, several cowboys stared open-mouthed at Eugenia, who smiled prettily. She didn't seem overly concerned to be traveling a great distance out in the open with an assemblage of ruffians. They would behave themselves, or else I would relieve them of their duties. My boys earned upwards of forty dollars a month, which was nothing to sneeze at.

"I see you found her," said Nelson Hardy, who approached. The tall, dark cowboy had been my right-hand man for the last two years. "I'll be…colored surprised. She's a beauty." Taking

Eugenia's hand, he assisted her to her feet.

"Thank you," she murmured.

Half the men were on horseback at a distance, but I addressed those that were near. "Boys, this is Sofia Parker, but she prefers to be called Eugenia. She's Mr. Hardin's fiancé. She'll be accompanying us to Kansas at Mr. Hardin's request. I hope you'll remember your manners where she's concerned."

Cook approached, eyeing us. "Say that again?" Apart from my position as trail boss, his was the next most respected, as he was second in command on the drive.

I pulled him aside, saying, "I got a telegram from Hardin. We're to escort his fiancé to Kansas." He gave me a look that spoke volumes. "I know, I know. It's not my idea of a good time, Marty."

"You got somethin' else to say to me?"

I sighed. "She's traveling with you."

He spat on the ground, scowling. "Tarnation!"

"I don't know what else to do. I suppose she could commandeer the supply wagon, but that was Randy's job. My back's up against the wall on this one. I don't like it either." I glanced over my shoulder, as the men had surrounded Eugenia, and, from the looks on their faces, they weren't all that disappointed to see her. One of them, Scott Fallen, had handed her a bushel of wildflowers that looked like Indian Blankets. Flabbergasted, I strode towards them, irritated beyond belief. "All right. Get back to work. We leave within the hour." Eugenia's expression stopped me in my tracks, because her smile was damnably infectious.

"Your men are very nice."

I ignored that. "I want you to meet cook. I'm not sure if you'll be riding with him or not."

"All right."

Marty was by my side, holding out a weathered hand. "Pleased to meet you, Miss Parker."

She shook it, smiling. "I'm happy to be here."

"You have any experience in making meals?"

"No, sir."

"You cook and clean?"

"I most certainly can. I wash clothes too."

His look of irritation lessened. "That's good news."

"I can learn to cook, sir. I'll do whatever I can to be helpful." She held out her hands, which were thin and lovely, but the nails were short and ragged. "I'm used to work."

Marty glanced at me. "We'll see how it goes. If she prattles incessantly, she's in the supply wagon."

I nodded, hating that I stared at Eugenia again, noting the look of concern on her face. "Fine. We'll take it a day at a time then."

"I can manage the supply wagon too, if you want. I don't mind traveling alone."

She was eager to please, and, perhaps, I had

misjudged her. She wasn't a frail, whimpering miss after all, but we hadn't even begun to move yet, and the road was difficult, even for the most seasoned cowboy. "I gotta make the rounds. We're off soon. We've wasted enough time."

"Yes, boss," said Marty. "Come with me, Eugenia. You can help pack the rest of the tins. I was almost done when you showed up."

"Certainly."

Removing my hat, I scratched my scalp, watching them wander towards the chuckwagon, which had been outfitted with heavy-duty running gear and wooden cabinets in the rear.

A voice behind me said, "That was not what I was expectin', boss."

I turned to find Nelson, who stood with his hands on his hips. "What?"

"She's stunning."

"She'll probably be cryin' the entire way to Kansas."

"Well, if she needs a shoulder to cry on…she can certainly have mine."

It rankled that my men were so easily besotted by a pretty face. "You'll be too busy workin' to have time for courtin' and all that nonsense."

"I'm mighty jealous of that old coot, Hardin. He may be rich, but she deserves better than that."

"Maybe all she cares about is his money? She'll be set up in a nice house with expensive things, waitin' for him to die. Then she'll be free to do as she wishes."

"Your opinion is awfully sour, Wyatt."

"Well," I kicked a stone, "I've seen enough to know most women are fickle and selfish. She's snagged herself a rich one. She'll be taken care of in style."

He whistled. "Who crossed you? I've never known you be such an old croaker."

"No one crossed me. I give her type a wide berth, is all. I prefer the "fallen frails" any day to the clingy ones who expect marriage. Plus, you know women are a bad omen on a cattle drive." His laughter was annoying.

"It's becoming clear now."

"What is?"

"You're not immune to the lovely Miss Parker. You're just as likely to fall for her as the rest of us. I don't think you've ever had one like this before."

I snorted. "You must still be drunk from last night."

"I'm as sober as the day I was born."

I patted him on the back. "Good. Let's saddle up and hit the road. We've got hours before sundown, and I want to make way."

"Yes, boss."

Five

I had never been received quite like this before. Every female instinct I possessed had savored the attention that had been lavished upon me by the cowboys. Even the cook, who wasn't overly pleased that I would be traveling with him, had softened noticeably. We sat together in the chuckwagon, which was drawn by a team of oxen. The men were behind us, circling the herd repeatedly, while encouraging the animals onward.

Not wanting to disturb Marty, I let my thoughts float in my mind, while we bounced and rattled across the plains, the pots and pans clanging. Marty enjoyed whistling, and he was quite proficient at it. I found myself tapping my toe to the lively tune. It being the first day on the trail, we would not stop until sunset, winding our way through miles of prairie. The cattle stretched out behind us in a long line, attended to by the cowboys, each man having a specific job. The drovers worked in pairs, while there were men in front and back. Wyatt Carson was a pointer, near the head, and I observed him several times during the day, riding to-and-fro.

The canvas top of the chuckwagon protected Marty and I from the heat, although it was sweltering nonetheless. My chemise was soaked through, as was the corset, which I vowed I would never wear again, until I reached civilization. The comfort of these garments was a concern, because I would be trapped in them for weeks. Marty was not fond of talking, preferring to chew tobacco, spitting it out occasionally. By the time the sun dipped, casting shadows around us, he began to speak.

"I gotta set up for dinner as soon as we stop."

"All right."

"I'll need you to find water. Can you do that?"

"I'll try my best."

He tugged on the reins, drawing the oxen to a slow, labored halt. "This will do." We were the first to arrive; the cowboys were far behind bringing up the herd. "This is pretty much how it's gonna go, honey. We start on fixin' dinner, while they come in."

Stepping from the wagon, I adjusted the bonnet. "Is there a bucket?"

"Absolutely." He jumped from the seat, hurrying towards the rear, where he tossed up the canvas, exposing a wooden cabinet. There were pots and pans and ladles hanging from hooks inside the wagon, along with crates and barrels of food stores. "Here you go. Mind your step."

"I will."

"I mean it. There are rattlesnakes out here. They don't want to be disturbed. If you hear a rattle, go in the other direction." He pointed to a line of bushes. "You might find water up around there."

"Yes, sir."

He'd tied an apron around his waist. "I gotta get the fire started."

My boots crunched over the rocky terrain, while I hunted for a creek or spring, not having a clue what I was looking for. The bushes yielded little, and, as I began to search further, the vastness of the surroundings overwhelmed me. Not wanting to disappoint Marty, I hurried forward, desperately needing to be useful.

"You lookin' for something?"

Startled, I glanced over my shoulder at a man on a horse. He had given me the flowers earlier in the day. "Water."

He pointed. "It's over there."

"Oh, thank you."

Grinning, he tipped his hat. "I'm happy to

oblige, ma'am."

"You saved me from wasting more time."

"You would've found it eventually." He prodded the horse with his heels. "You be careful now, ya hear?"

"I will." He was gone a second later, disappearing across the field. When I returned with a full bucket, Marty had a hearty fire blazing, while he chopped meat on a wooden board. He worked from the back of the wagon, as the fold-down door functioned like a table. "What can I do?"

He held up a sizable lump of dough. "I need these made into balls and baked in the Dutch oven. When they're done, they should look like this." He tossed something my way, and I caught it. "That's a sourdough biscuit."

I sniffed it, inhaling the scent of yeast. "I can do that."

"Good."

"What's for supper?"

"Pot roast with potatoes. The boys will want coffee too."

While I worked on making the biscuits, he labored over the table, chopping and cutting, until everything went into a huge pot over the fire. It smelled heavenly, with a hint of onion and garlic. I worried that I would spoil the biscuits by not arranging or baking them properly, but the white lumps rose and browned beautifully.

By the time the cattle had been brought in, the men descended upon camp, most carrying bedrolls. The sunset cast streaks of purple and orange across the sky, the sun dipping lower by the second. There was talking and laughter, while some of the men disappeared into the prairie to find the creek and scrub away hours of dirt after a dusty day of riding. Not having brought a bedroll, I wondered where I would sleep.

"So, how'd she do?" Wyatt sauntered over; his grin was friendly, yet inquisitive. "Did she talk your ear off?"

Marty held a dozen or more tin plates. "Not at all. Not a peep outta her all day."

Mr. Carson did not seem to have anything to say about that, staring at me peculiarly. I had removed the bonnet, because I no longer needed it to protect myself from the sun. "Supper's almost ready."

"I can smell it. Marty makes the best short ribs in the state."

"Boss!"

"Yeah?"

One of his men approached. "A calf was born."

He took the news pragmatically. "All right. It's gonna have to travel by wagon tomorrow."

I found that strange. "Why can't it be with its mother?"

"It won't be able to keep up. They gotta be transported in separate sacks, so the mom will know the smell of her baby when they're reunited in the evening. The baby can feed all night."

"What happens without the sacks?"

"The mothers get all confused."

"It's better than the alternative," said Marty. "Calves are usually slaughtered, cause they're just too darn slow."

"Then I'm grateful that won't happen." There was something about Wyatt that appealed to me, and it was a pleasure to be in his company, although his demeanor was somewhat prickly. He didn't want to like me, but I sensed he did. "Can I ask you something, sir?"

"No, sir, just Wyatt, but yeah?"

"I didn't bring a bedroll."

"That's all right, sweetheart," said Scott Fallen, who had joined us by the chuckwagon. "She can share mine." He had been the same cowboy who had given me the wildflowers earlier.

Wyatt's scowl was one for the record books. His eyes had closed to slits, while two deep lines appeared between them. "I don't think Mr. Hardin would be too pleased with that type of arrangement. This is his fiancé, after all, and you've just disrespected her with your immoral proposition."

"I'm sorry." He grinned contritely. "Please

accept my heartfelt apology. I'm a…numbskull cowboy. What can I say?"

I wasn't offended at all, feeling flattered, because I knew he jested. Wyatt's reaction had been interesting. "Apology accepted."

"But, if you decide you don't wanna marry Mr—" Wyatt began to push him, "I'd be more than happy to offer for you."

"Out you go!"

"Aw, come on," he laughed. "I was only making time with the pretty lady."

"Go charm the roots off that bush over there."

"Here you go, Wyatt." Marty handed him a shiny tin plate. "You can start ladlin' out however much you want. The biscuits are in the basket."

"Thank you."

Everyone settled down to eat, their plates brimming with steaming chunks of meat in a hearty sauce with potatoes and biscuits. I ate my fill, finding Marty's cooking surprisingly delicious. He was better than most chefs at restaurants. After everyone had eaten, I collected the plates, wanting to be helpful and wash them. A day of work on the trail was far easier than doing laundry. Memories of scrubbing linen over a washboard with abrasive soap flitted through my mind. This was done for hours, bent over a vat of water, while my back ached and my arms throbbed. If helping to prepare supper and washing dishes was all that was required of me, this was heaven!

The only regret was Sofia, who I had wronged in death, not telling anyone about her passing. I prayed she was in a better place now. I had stolen her things and her name, staking a future for myself, which seemed infinitely more promising than the life I had known before. Yet, guilt still needled me.

After the dishes were washed and put away, the men reclined on their bedrolls around the fire, while smoking cigarettes and drinking coffee. Someone played the harmonica; the tune was slightly melancholy. I sat on a rock, holding my lower back, wishing I could remove the corset. I would sleep in these clothes, but something had to be done to ease the discomfort.

"Here." A bundle came my way, landing at my feet. "A bed for you."

"Thank you, Wyatt."

Laughter from the chuckwagon reached us, as Marty and another man talked. "I'll be back."

I eyed his departure, admiring the way his pants fit in the seat. Trying not to focus on such thoughts, I unrolled the bed, finding a canvas lining with a thin blanket and pillow. It would be hard and uncomfortable, but it was a luxury nonetheless. Once my things had been arranged, I set out to divest myself of the corset, vowing to shove the item into the bottom of my bag for the duration of the cattle drive.

Behind a bush in the distance, I unbuttoned the fitted top, exposing my arms and neck, while working to loosen the corset. Once free, I donned the bodice again, feeling instant relief. Tucking the corset into the bag, I dragged it with me, depositing it inside the spare wagon.

"Good riddance to you," I murmured.

Needing to wash, I strode towards the water source, finding several men loitering. They had brought a lantern, which cast a fair amount of light across the placid water. A man was in the stream, standing mid waist, entirely naked. I gasped, turning from him, only to face Wyatt, who grinned sardonically.

"If you're gonna wander around at night, you're gonna see things like that."

"It's all right," I giggled, while tamping down a wave of embarrassment. "It looks refreshing. I'm sorely tempted to do the same."

Something darkened in his look, the grin vanishing. "That sure would be a sight."

A heady energy skimmed down my backbone, producing pleasurable tingles in my belly. Our eyes locked, while the men carried on, laughing and splashing. I was at a loss for a long, yet breathless moment, drawn to him and fascinated by the way I felt in his presence. The silence wasn't awkward in the least.

"I'm sorry," he murmured. "I shouldn't have said that. I think we're all gonna have to remember our manners around you." Without another word, he strode away, disappearing into the darkness.

I wished he had stayed longer.

Six

I thought Eugenia would be difficult to manage, mostly because she was female, but, as the days wore on and she acclimated, not only did she thrive, but her efforts had earned the admiration and respect of the men. Marty said she had never complained once and he appreciated her cooking and cleaning efforts. She had even taken in laundry one evening, scrubbing and wringing for hours, while we slept. Clean clothing on the trail was almost unheard of, but the men sported freshly laundered duds every four or five days.

The first evening, Eugenia had placed her bedroll across the campfire. On the second night, she was two over to the right, and on the third, five, until she had worked her way all around the circle, settling in next to me. Most of the men kept the same spots, even after changing locations, as they tended to be near those men they enjoyed talking to. Knowing that she was edging closer every night, it set up a compelling sense of expectancy. Being only inches away from her, left me restless and distracted, almost as if I had drunk too much coffee.

We had finished supper an hour ago, and Eugenia had taken the plates to the river, as we had been following it for days. I typically shadowed her, worrying that she might encounter wildlife or one of the boys, who, after two weeks on the trail, eyed her with interest, raw need etched into their features. We would be near a town tomorrow, and they were eager to cut loose and indulge in whiskey and women, but first we had to get through the night. Female humming caught my attention, while I surefooted it through the bushes, emerging near the water's edge. The full moon provided a fair amount of light, the surface of the river shimmering.

Amidst the sounds of crickets and trickling water, a woman bathed, although only her shoulders were above the surface, but her skin was hidden beneath a white chemise. "How is it?"

She stiffened, turning towards me. "Fine. Cold, but fine."

"Looks like you found the deepest spot."

"I did. I wish I knew what I was stepping on, though."

"Is it slimy?"

"No, just sharp."

"Don't hurt yourself." I had knelt, sitting on the rocks, while eyeing her.

"Are you going to watch me?" Her dark, wet hair clung to her back.

"It's my job to make sure you're safe."

Her smile was saucy. "Are you behaving yourself, Mr. Carson?"

"Not normally." She had grown into a flirt, but my boys were to blame, as they lavished her with far too much attention.

"You can't see anything, can you?"

"Nope," I lied.

"I think you're fibbing."

"A cowboy always tells the truth." The sound of a harmonica echoed from the nearby camp, while men laughed.

She dunked her head back, exposing the whiteness of her neck. "I'm almost finished." Pulling her hair to the side, she rung out water from the long tresses, while moving slowly in my direction. "Are you sure you can't see anything?"

"You're fully covered."

Yet, as she emerged, every curve and indentation was revealed, because the cloth clung to her like a second skin. It was almost worse than being naked. I longed to know what those breasts looked like, seeing the precise outlines, with the jutting peaks of her nipples pressing against the garment. In a fit of irritation, I jumped to my feet, knowing I could not stay another moment. It had been a mistake to watch her.

At camp, the men sat around the fire singing "In The Sweet By and By", while Judd played the harmonica. They were eager for a night on the town, as was I, but I worried about Eugenia and her safety, while we cut loose for the night. She emerged from the bushes a while later with wet hair, a slight smile lifting the edges of her mouth. I hated that I knew exactly what she looked like, what fine, shapely curves lay beneath the dress she wore. It was an intimate knowledge reserved only for husbands, and I would never be able to erase it from my mind. It would fuel an endless amount of fantasies.

She sat on a bedroll, running fingers through her hair, while staring into the fire. I admired the side of her face, the pert nose and slightly pointy chin. Something was on her mind; her gaze seemed focused and thoughtful. It had been a long, hard day, having to stop to collect three calves that had arrived earlier, holding up the drive. Then an afternoon storm had sent us into rescue mode, while trying to prevent the cattle from stampeding because of the lightning. I was sore from my tailbone all the way to the top of my head.

Sensing my attention, she glanced at me. While

the boys sang and laughed, our eyes met, and an inexplicable fire began to simmer, which I had felt from day one. She tended to her hair, working out the tangles, the strands hanging down her back, nearly to her bottom. Her grooming habits were duly noted, as I was not the only one enthralled by her. Scott Fallen sang, but his attention wasn't on the music; he watched Eugenia as well, his eyes glinting with a carnal light.

Once the fire had died down, the harmonica was put away, and the boys settled. Someone slept already, because the sound of snoring filled the air. Exhausted after a wearying day, I turned to my side, adjusting the pillow beneath my head. Eugenia and I were less than two feet apart, but the distance was easily breached. The temptation was nearly overwhelming. If she wasn't the bosses' fiancé, I knew what I would do, but I would hate myself for it. Those lips begged for kissing, and I yearned to be the one to taste them, rather than someone like Scott Fallen, whom I had begun to loathe.

"Is he a nice man?" she whispered.

Confused, I asked, "What?"

"Mr. Hardin?"

"I've no idea."

"What's his reputation like?"

"He's an astute businessman."

"Was he ever married?"

This was a strange question, as she should know. "Isn't that in the letters?"

"His penmanship is dreadful. I'm not the best reader anyhow, but it's hard to make out."

"He had two wives. They both died."

"Really?"

"One at childbirth and another from some accident." She did not seem to like this bit of news.

"How old is he?"

"Late forties."

"How old are you?"

"Thirty." I grinned. "Too old too, huh?"

"Not at all. I'd rather have thirty than forty."

"What's your age?"

"Eighteen."

"You lived in Texas your whole life?"

"Yes."

"What did you do in San Antonio?"

"My mother was a prostitute. I was raised in a brothel."

I had not been expecting that. "You don't say."

"She was a partner with the madam. We had our own room, so it wasn't all that bad. I didn't see anything, if that's what that look is about."

"What look?"

"You think I'm loose now, don't you?"

"No. I know you're not. I knew the moment I met you."

"You did?"

"You got nothin' to worry about there. I'm not in the habit of taking advantage of innocent women." Disappointment registered on her face, but it vanished in a flash.

"I don't want that life. I want a husband and children and peace and quiet. A farm would be nice too."

I lay on my back, staring at the stars. "Sounds like a noose around the neck."

"What?"

"You'll find all that with Mr. Hardin. A match made in heaven."

"Is wanting to settle down a crime?"

"For me it is." I tilted my head in her direction. She lay on her side, with her hand beneath her cheek. It was always a mistake to look at her. She looked so sweet and vulnerable in that instant.

"What if I don't like him?"

"You've been corresponding for months, I presume. You should know his character."

"From letters?" she laughed quietly. "You can't get that from a letter, Mr. Carson. You have to spend time with someone to know that."

"That's why the mail order business is plain stupid."

"Scott said your brothers found wives that way."

"He has a big mouth."

"He said your mother is quite a character."

"He don't know what he's talkin' about."

"Are you always so guarded?"

"What do you mean?"

"You never say anything about yourself."

"Most men don't. It's boring conversation."

"I told you about my upbringing. I probably should've kept it quiet."

"You've had a rough life, Eugenia."

"So have you."

She had me stumped there.

"You carry a lot of it on your shoulders. Nelsen was saying you've done a fair amount of thieving and cattle rustling."

"Everybody needs to quit talkin'," I grumbled.

"It's not their fault." She leaned nearer, her gaze straying to my mouth. "I asked them about you."

"You should go to sleep. We're keepin' people up. We gotta get an early start tomorrow." Her words bothered me on several levels.

"Mr. Carson?"

"What?"

"I don't know you at all, but I like you. I know you saw me nearly naked, but I'm not angry about it."

"Now *you* need to quit talkin'."

She smiled shyly, her expression flirtatious. "Might I come to town with you tomorrow?"

"Absolutely not."

"Why?"

"Cause the men will be drunk and on the prowl for whores." I regretted speaking so plainly. "I mean, lookin' for a good time."

"What will I do?"

"Stay at camp. I'll leave a rifle with you."

"I don't know how to shoot."

"A revolver then."

"I've never shot that either."

Anger flared, as she had thoroughly gotten under my skin. "Go to sleep, Eugenia."

"Maybe you could stay with me, while they go to town. You could watch over me."

My heart pounded in my chest at the implication of her words. Being alone with her all night would lead to trouble, because I doubted I would be able to resist her. It took everything I had not to reach out and grab her now. Grasping the blanket, I turned, presenting my back.

"Good night, Eugenia."

"Good night, Wyatt."

Sleep was elusive, as unbidden images drifted through my mind, leaving me heated to the core, while beads of sweat broke out on my forehead. *The little minx!*

Seven

A noise woke me in the middle of the night, and I turned to look at Wyatt, noting an empty bedroll. He stood nearby checking his weapon. Sitting, I gazed at the camp, the smoldering fire, and the men that slept, although several had gotten to their feet.

"What's the matter?"

"You stay here, honey." He slid the revolver into the holster at his side. "We suspect rustlers are tryin' to snatch a coupla head. Gotta put a stop to it."

"Is that dangerous?" The thought of him being shot concerned me.

"Yeah, but you've got nothin' to worry about."

I bit my lip. "Please be careful."

"I do this for a livin'." He grinned crookedly. "I might've rustled a few cattle in my time too."

"We better skedaddle," said Nelson. "Time's a wastin'."

Shep Selman pulled a boot on. "Go on! I'll follow."

Six of the men departed, while the rest stayed behind, lying on their bedrolls, oblivious to the commotion. Sleep was almost impossible to come by, once they had gone. After a series of shots were fired, echoing in the distance, I gave up entirely, as had some of the other cowboys, who had woken. Marty tossed wood in the fire, making a pot of hot chocolate, which was much appreciated. We sat and waited for the news, while staring at the flames and sipping our drinks. It seemed like an eternity before Wyatt and his men returned, and, when they did, the camp was in utter chaos.

"Scott's been shot!" said Shep.

Marty sprang to action, approaching the wounded man on his horse. "How are you, son?"

"It's my arm. I'll live."

"Did the bullet go through?"

"Yeah."

"All right. Come on down. I'll take a look at it."

I scanned the men, searching for Wyatt, who brought up the rear. Hurrying to him, I asked, "What happened?"

"Aw, nothin'. The usual."

"Was it rustlers?"

"It was."

"And they're gone now?"

"You could say that."

"They're dead?"

"They will be soon."

"Goodness."

"Stealin' cattle's a serious offense. We don't take too kindly to it. Them boys knew what they were doin'." He placed his hands on his hips. "I gotta clean up and get some shuteye."

He seemed perfectly fine, but dirty, as dust coated his face. This business was far more dangerous than I thought. Somewhere out on the plains, men were wounded and dying.

Scott Fallen was being seen to by Marty, and I approached. "Can I help?" The young cowboy had taken his shirt off, revealing a tapered and toned chest that was smattered with light brown hair.

"Gotta clean the wound." He poured a splash of whiskey, which he kept for medicinal purposes. "It needs a coupla stitches."

Scott's grin was impish. "I'm better now that Eugenia's here."

I knelt beside him, while he sat on a crate. "Did it really go all the way through?"

"It did."

"Does that hurt?"

"Aw…not that bad."

Marty snorted. "You boys lie through your teeth just to impress the ladies. It burns like heck, honey."

"You could've been killed."

"Yes, ma'am. Hazards of the job."

"Won't your family miss you?"

"Surely, but I'm not married…yet."

Marty threaded a needle. "Hold still for a second, son."

I glanced over my shoulder, seeing Wyatt, who had returned. He seemed to scowl in my direction, staring at us. "Well, it looks like you're managing just fine. I'm off to bed. It's been an exciting evening, fellas."

"Don't leave." Scott grasped my hand. "Lookin' at you makes me feel better. You sure are pretty."

I demurred. "Oh…stop that."

"It's true. Isn't she pretty, Marty? I'm not lying."

"She is, but she's taken, and you'd be good to remember that. She's the boss' fiancé."

"It's a long drive to Kansas. I might be able to persuade her to marry me instead."

I got to my feet. "Well, you're very bold, Mr. Fallen. I think I had better watch myself around you." Those words were spoken in jest, but they sounded terribly flirtatious. I had never been so forward when it came to men. I had grown more at ease around them from the days spent on the trail, and we frequently laughed about humorous stories. I enjoyed flirting with them, as it was harmless.

When I returned to the bedroll, Wyatt had settled next to me. "Are you finished holding his hand?"

"Pardon?" I began to remove my boots, while staring at him. He had washed his face in the river, and his hair was wet.

"My boys don't need a woman to coddle 'em."

Was he jealous? "I wasn't coddling him. I was trying to be helpful. If you had a bullet through your arm, I would've offered assistance."

He muttered something under his breath. The camp had settled down again, the men snoring, while Marty and Scott talked softly by the chuckwagon.

"What happened?" I settled beneath the blanket, facing Wyatt.

"Rustlers rounded up about twenty head, hiding in a ravine. Nifty trick, but it didn't work. We flushed 'em out."

"How did you know they were there?"

"The junior cowboys were on the night watch. They came back to tell us."

"Will this happen often?"

"Maybe, maybe not."

"Would they come here?"

"Not those boys." He yawned, falling onto his

back. "I gotta sleep, honey. I'm exhausted."

"Good night, Wyatt."

"Good night, Eugenia."

I loved the sound of my name on his lips. The dying fire cast shadows across the camp, as the men slept. We would all be tired tomorrow for having our rest interrupted. As I lay my head on the pillow, I stared at Wyatt for a long time, admiring his profile, as I did often. There wasn't anything about him that I disliked, finding him handsome and fascinating. I stared, until my lids grew so heavy they closed.

In the morning, the sounds of talking and laughter resonated along with the aroma of coffee and bacon. Marty had made a hearty breakfast, as was expected of the first meal of the day. Sliding on my boots, I left the bedding, taking a moment to roll it up, bringing it with me to the supply wagon, where the others had been deposited. When I had made myself presentable, washing by the river and changing into a somewhat clean dress, I joined everyone around the chuckwagon.

Scott grinned, ambling over. "Aren't you a sight for sore eyes."

"Oh, stop that." He knelt beside me, as I sat on a crate.

"Don't you wanna know how I am?"

"You look the picture of health."

He nodded. "I am, but only because you're the

best medicine a man could have."

"Now I know you're fibbing."

"All right," said Shep. "Finish up here. We're headin' out. Somebody's gotta grab the calves. Then we're on our way."

The camp sprang to life, as men hurried back and forth, and Marty began to put things away. "I need to help." I had barely had enough time to eat, having slept too long.

Once we were on our way, I sat with Marty, while he commandeered the oxen, encouraging them onward. Our wagon rattled, being jostled back and forth over the rough terrain. It was similar to all the other days spent driving, while the men were behind us, bringing up the line of cows that stretched for a mile or two, the stragglers coming in last.

By lunchtime, we were situated near the base of a rugged, jutting mountain, where we made a fire for the noon meal. The Dutch oven baked biscuits, while Marty fried steaks and boiled beans. After everyone had eaten, we napped, letting the animals graze longer. They walked for twelve to fifteen miles a day, and, if they weren't allowed to eat well, they'd lose too much weight, lessening their value.

Finding shade was a challenge, while the midday sun was at its hottest. Several men crawled beneath the chuckwagon to sleep, while others were under the supply wagon. I sat by a tree and dozed, my head drifting from side to side. It was a lazy, humid day, with the threat of an afternoon rainstorm brewing in the distance, the clouds gathering and growing. Once we had woken, Marty and I were the first on the road, ambling ahead, while the cowboys plodded along behind us. The slow and steady march brought us around the mountain, following a verdant gully between the peaks.

I sweltered in the heat; my chest damp with perspiration. Marty whistled and chewed tobacco, spitting periodically. He hated senseless chatter, so I kept my thoughts to myself, but my mind was active. I thought of Sofia often, aware that she had been my age, and now she was gone. Everyone I knew had perished far too soon, leading me to question my own longevity. My mother's illness had left her neck swollen, and she had been unable to breathe. Several of the prostitutes had fallen victim at the same time, and I worried I would too, but God had been merciful. I wasn't prone to prayer, my mother having hated church, as harlots were generally shunned among the population, but a part of me longed to listen to a sermon or two. I craved normality and a place to live where I could grow a vegetable garden. It would be a dream to have children, which I would happily take to church every Sunday, garbed in their best outfits, the girls in straw bonnets. I had craved respectability ever since I could remember. I wondered if Mr. Hardin was amiable to such things. In his letters, he had spoken of having a large house, and I had assumed a man of his stature would attend church and social functions regularly.

He would be able to provide the life I had always dreamed of…but would I love him?

Eight

The boys were restless, and, knowing that the town of Wally was near, they were fair to bursting to leave work for a good time. We had stopped for camp, and, while Marty began dinner preparations, the lights of Wally glowed in the distance like sinful beacons. An air of expectancy lingered; the vibration was celebratory in nature and slightly wild. They would raise hell once they hit the streets, even before indulging in whiskey.

I would normally be just as eager, but the thought of Eugenia alone seemed to dampen my enthusiasm. I had given her a loaded pistol, showing her how to use it, but she had seemed hesitant, almost anxious, and I knew she was worried about being left alone. But the boys expected me to join them, and I was eager to cut loose as well, bending an elbow at the bar. The memory of her nearly naked had left me wound up tighter than a Texas T knot. Only the services of a "fair belle" could put out those flames. Maybe, after, I'd be able to think straight again.

"Well, boys," I said, grinning, "once we've eaten, we can ride over to town." A chorus of voices chimed in agreement.

"Amen!" said one of the younger cowboys. "I'm ready for a little who-hit-John tonight. Yes, sir."

Eugenia sat on her bedroll, with her arms around her knees, staring into the fire. The revolver was on the ground next to her, looking out of place. I gazed at her, admiring the curve of her face and the way her lashes cast shadows upon her cheeks. She had been an asset to the group, working tirelessly by Marty's side, never complaining.

After cleaning up by the river, the men began to file out. I had freshened up, wearing a clean shirt and bandana, but I was reluctant to leave. Approaching Eugenia, she glanced up at me. "You gonna be all right, honey?"

"I'm fine." Her smile was tremulous. "You go and enjoy yourselves. I just hope you find your way back."

She looked vulnerable and small sitting there, with her long, nearly black hair hanging down her back. I knelt, staring at her, which seemed to surprise her, as her eyes widened. "If you hear anything, fire a shot in the air, and I'll come runnin'."

"I'm going to sleep soon. I…might sleep in the supply wagon."

"It smells of cow, honey. You don't want to sleep there."

"Hey, Wyatt!" shouted Shep. "We're goin' to the burg now. Let's hit the road."

She pushed me gently. "Go. I want to hear all about it when you get back."

A hand was on my shoulder. "Come on boss, we know you're sweet on the pretty lady, but we gotta go."

It was irritating having my men speak in this manner, but it had been the truth. The cure for my predicament was drink and women, both of which I planned to indulge in with impunity. Getting to my feet, I resolved not to think about Eugenia again, wanting and needing a distraction. Without looking back, I met up with Nelson and Shep, while the others had already departed.

"All right." I stepped in the stirrup, flinging a leg over the horse. "Let's have us a hog-killin' time, boys." A cacophony of shouts rang out, while we spurred our horses into a gallop.

We closed the distance in less than ten minutes, the lights of Wally shining brightly. The town spanned from one end of a dusty boardwalk to the other, with a variety of establishments on either side, but most were closed at this time of night. Only the saloon and the brothel welcomed patrons, all of whom were men. We tied the horses to the hitching post out front. I followed, sauntering towards the doors, while casting a glance around. Having been on the wrong side of the law for quite a few years, I had an intuitive feeling for trouble, recognizing a desperado when I saw one, but no one made me look twice.

"Here he is," said Marty. "Took you long enough."

I sat in the stool next to him, while the bartender slid a glass my way. I didn't have to ask, so he poured whiskey, nodding. "Thank you."

"You boys on a drive?"

"Yes, we are."

"From San Antonio?"

"Yep." I took a sip, the fluid burning a path straight into my belly. "Ah…that's good." A commotion over my shoulder had me glancing in that direction, seeing Scott Fallen with a saloon girl on his lap. She was tossing her boa around his neck flirtatiously.

Several of my men had sat at tables to play cards, which wasn't a half bad idea, but I tended to lose badly. They would blow their wages for the month, if they weren't careful. Nursing the whiskey, I savored each sip, not wanting to imbibe too freely, as I sensed I might be called upon later to break up a fight or two. These boys had been together for weeks, and resentments had been simmering, as there had been arguments. Once alcohol was added to the equation, they were likely to fight like Kilkenny cats, if left to their own devices.

An hour later, I was ready for other amusements, wanting to take a stroll towards the parlour house with Nelson in tow. The boys were holding their own, and Marty would intervene, if necessary. A sense of anticipation put a spring to my step, my boots clopping on the wooden platform. Flush with whiskey and feeling no pain, I longed to meet a comely young thing who would offer up a diversion for an hour or so. Once through the doorway, a plush, yet smoky environment greeted us, as men milled about and women flirted.

Nelson and I took up a position against the wall, while a woman brought over drinks. Her cleavage bulged from the top of the corset. "Hello, fellas."

"Hi, honey," said Nelson, his gaze lowering. "I think I like what's on the menu."

I took the glass from her. "Thank you."

"Is there anything in particular you're looking for tonight?" she purred.

"I'll know it when I see it," I said.

"We've some new girls from Houston. I think you'll like them."

A woman strolled towards us, passing, while leaving a cloud of cheap perfume in her wake. A seat became available, and I lowered myself onto the sofa, reclining. Scanning the room, nothing caught my eye, which was unusual. Nelson was in conversation with a redhead, although I doubted the color was real, while Shep had just arrived, bringing with him two of the younger cowboys. It was amusing watching them, as they stared wide-eyed at the women. Their inexperience would make them easy prey, as they would both be overcharged.

Finding the goings-on mildly fascinating, I observed each of the boys and their reactions, especially right before they were led upstairs, taken by the hand by two different women. Those harlots had worn face paint and revealing clothing, their appearances garish. I preferred the simpler, more natural girls, but they were few and far between. While thus occupied, my mind was filled with images of Eugenia, and I couldn't help wondering about her safety.

A hand on my shoulder snapped me out of this daydream. I turned to find Marty. "There's trouble, boss."

"Is Eugenia all right?"

He blinked, shaking his head. "It's not her. It's

a fight. Somebody's gotta break it up."

"That figures." I got to my feet.

We hurried from the establishment, towards several men throwing fists in the road, two of whom were my boys. Marty and I interjected ourselves into the skirmish, he grabbing Duncan, while I held onto John. Both of them were unsteady on their feet, having consumed too much whiskey.

"Let's cool off for a spell," I said. "Why don't you go back to the saloon, eh? Before you break an arm or somethin'."

Marty fingered his gun, glaring at the other wranglers. "It's over."

"They started it," griped a man in a top hat.

"It don't matter," I muttered.

John brushed dirt off his trousers. "I'm gonna pretend you didn't call my mother a whore."

I grabbed him, pushing him towards the batwing doors of the saloon, before they went at each other again. "That's enough. He's not worth your spit, son."

Marty was behind me. "That's right. Don't let one blowhard spoil a good time. There's a whiskey with my name on it somewhere."

After things had settled and the men were well into their cups, the urge to return to camp had me reaching for my hat.

"Where you goin'?" slurred Marty.

"I'm checkin' on Miss Parker."

He grinned lopsidedly. "Oh, I bet. That pretty girl left all alone." He clucked. "She's waiting on you, no doubt."

"What's that supposed to mean?"

"Come on. You're hopin' she'll change her mind and marry you instead. It wouldn't be such a hardship settling down with her. I've spent more time in her company than any man here. She's easy to travel with and a hard worker. A woman like that would run a fine household and keep them children in line."

"You of all people know I ain't lookin' to settle down. I'd prefer a noose around my neck before the shackles of domesticity." His laughter grated on my nerves.

"All right. You're not willin' to admit to anything yet, but I bet by the time we arrive in Abilene, you'll be singin' a different tune."

Irritated, I scowled at him, placing my hat on my head. "I'll be back to check on things. None of 'em are gettin' any soberer."

"Nope. They'll be feelin' swell tomorrow," he chuckled.

I left without preamble, striding from the establishment towards my horse. Once mounted and on the road, I encouraged her into a gallop, not wanting to waste another moment. I had not fully indulged in the pleasure of town, as I should have, my mind occupied with a raven-haired vixen, who waited alone by a dying fire. I hadn't heard a shot, so I assumed all was well, but she had to be frightened. Cutting a line straight to where the wagons were, I glimpsed a figure standing by the chuckwagon. Eager to see how Eugenia had fared, I dismounted, striding towards her.

Her smile was fragile, yet appreciative. "You didn't have to check on me."

I scanned her person from head to foot, noting she wore a practical calico dress and boots. Having been keen to see her, it wasn't surprising that I took her into my arms. She felt exactly like I had imagined, slight yet strong, her hands snaking around my neck. Holding her face, my attention drifted to her mouth, which was partially open, revealing white, even teeth. I hadn't meant to take such liberties, but I knew when a woman wanted me, and, when I felt the same, it was almost impossible to resist. I'd known it from the first moment I had met her.

"Eugenia?"

"Yes?" she breathed.

"I'm gonna kiss you."

Something indefinable flared in her eyes. "I hoped you would."

Nine

The last three hours had been nerve-wracking. I would never tell the men, but I had been terrified to be left alone, even with a loaded pistol nearby. The rustling of the wind and the howl of coyotes had me glancing around, fearing that an animal would invade the camp and attack me. At one point I had sat in the chuckwagon, but it was crowded with crates and provisions.

I had perceived the horse at a distance, and a part of me had prayed that it was Wyatt. Once he had come into view, my heart leapt with joy. We were the only ones here now…the possibility of knowing him better had presented itself, and, as he had approached, the only thought I had was of kissing him. He had taken me into his arms. He was going to kiss me, his lips nearing mine, when a shout rang out, followed by raucous laughter.

"Blasted heck!" he muttered, dropping his hands.

Several horses had arrived, carrying drunken cowboys, who fell to their feet and struggled to get up again. Others staggered to the fire, laughing and slurring their words. The moment was shattered, my disappointment acute, but I took his hand boldly, leading him away. Someone had brought back a bottle of whiskey.

"Hey," called Wyatt. "That's not allowed, and you know it. No spirits at camp."

"Aw, come on, boss. Just for tonight? Please?"

His brows had furrowed. "We're hittin' the road early tomorrow. You boys better be up and sober by then."

"Yes, boss."

More riders were on the way, the remaining men fast approaching. I sighed. "Well, that was timely." My frustration was evident. I had yet to let go of his hand.

"Honey, this was a bad idea anyway." He touched my face. "You're the boss' fiancé and strictly off-limits. I gotta check on my men. They were rowdy as heck. Gotta make sure nobody is missin'." Regret shone in his eyes.

We wouldn't have a single moment alone.

"Don't look at me like that."

"Like what?"

"Like you are now."

"You're my favorite cowboy."

He kicked a stone, mumbling something under his breath. "Keep your opinions to yourself, you hear?" He pressed a finger to my mouth. "Not another word." With that, he sauntered off, muttering to himself.

I took stock of the situation, knowing I had been too forward, but I would never regret those words. With a heavy heart, I returned to the fire, where several men had fallen to their bedrolls, sleeping off the effects of the liquor. Marty had returned and placed a pot on the coals, tossing in pieces of meat, onions, and eggs, producing a quick and easy meal.

He said, "This will help soak up some of the booze."

With reluctance, I sat on my bedding, removing my boots, while hoping that Wyatt would place his bedroll next to mine. He had gone off somewhere, but I heard talking in the distance. When he returned, I was beneath the blanket watching him. It was another hour before he joined me, tossing down the bedroll and removing his boots. The men ate and talked for a while, but they eventually quieted. Sleep was not easy to come by, and, after an hour, I finally dozed. At some point during the night, the feel of something wet hit my face. Sitting up, I observed the fire smoking, while listening to the snores of several men. The wetness was from rain, and it had begun to fall harder.

"Drats," I muttered. We would all be soaked within ten minutes. Wyatt must have perceived me, because he sat up, touching his face. I glanced at him. "We'll be wet."

"Yeah," he murmured. Getting to his feet, he motioned to me. "Come here."

Not knowing what he intended, I stood watching him, while he dragged the bottom portion of the canvas from my bed over to his. Tossing my pillow onto the bedding, he motioned. "Come on."

I approached, as my heart beat a wild staccato, knowing that we would be sleeping together. I slid beneath his blankets, while he did the same, tossing my canvas over our heads, which insulated us from the rain. There wasn't an inch between us, so I turned into him, pressing my nose to his shoulder. Taking advantage of the situation, I placed an arm over his belly, while my leg captured his.

"That's close enough, honey."

"Will it rain all night?"

"Hard to say."

I touched his chin, feeling the abrasive quality of manly stubble. "The men will be soaked through."

"It's their own darn fault for gettin' so drunk."

"I thought you'd be drunker."

"I guess I didn't it enjoy it as much as I wanted to."

"I'm really happy it rained."

"Shush."

"I hope it rains all night." He took my hand, squeezing it, as if he didn't want me to touch him.

"Go to sleep."

"I've never shared a bed with a man before."

He growled deep in his chest. "If you can't quit your gibbering—"

"You owe me a kiss. You said you were going to kiss me."

His hand went over my mouth. "Marty said you were the quiet type. Now shush." I licked his fingers. "Stop that."

"You taste salty."

He turned suddenly, grabbing me so I faced away from him. A steely arm went around my midsection. "Not another word," he warned near my ear. His heated breath sent a shiver down my spine.

"Oh, fine." It was wonderful being this close to him; his arm was around my abdomen in a possessive manner. I sighed, closing my eyes, while the sound of rain pelted the canvas over my head. "Good night, Wyatt."

"Night, Eugenia."

In the morning, I found myself snuggled next

to something warm, while pots and pans clanked and rattled. Marty was awake. I had slept like a baby, not waking once, until now. Snores continued to resonate, and Wyatt was out completely.

Someone sneezed then. "Jeez…I'm all wet. Everything's soaked."

"Yeah," muttered another man. "They were smart."

He was referring to Wyatt and me, as we had used my canvas for protection from the elements. "Looks awfully cozy over there."

"He's takin' *real* good care of the boss' fiancé."

Tossing the canvas aside, I glared at the person who I thought had spoken. "Oh, pipe down." Getting to my feet, I stomped across camp, determined to find a private spot to use the privy.

Before I was out of earshot, I heard, "She's pretty, even when she's mad."

"Heck, if I'd been next to her, I would've done the same."

'Wyatt's a lucky cuss."

Not wanting to listen to gossip, I continued to the creek, bending to cleanse my face and hands. I'd had one of the most astonishing nights of my life, sleeping in the arms of a man I greatly admired and thought handsome. He said he would kiss me, he had meant to, but we had been interrupted. I would have given myself to him, if we had been alone. While I sat by the water's edge, I pondered these feelings, realizing that they ran far deeper than I had imagined.

"There you are."

I glanced over my shoulder, as Wyatt approached, which gave me a thrill. "Thank you for last night."

He knelt beside me, cupping water in his hands. "We had no choice. It was better than catching cold. My boys are gonna be sick in a day or two." He scrubbed his face, using a finger to brush his teeth, rinsing and gurgling with the water.

"I hope it rains every night."

Wyatt ignored that remark, tossing water over his neck. When he had finished, he glanced at me, and I thought he would say something, but whatever it was seemed to die on his lips.

"I have to tell you something."

"What?" He sat next to me, drawing his knees up.

"I'm not Miss Parker."

"Pardon?"

"That's not my name."

"Then who the heck are you?"

"Sofia Parker was my roommate. She died a day before you arrived in San Antonio."

His mouth fell open. "What…"

"I took her place. I read the letters, well, most of them. Then I pretended to be her."

"What's your name?"

"Eugenia Madsen."

"I'm not sure why you're tellin' me this."

"I'm not a mail order bride, Wyatt. Sofia was. It was her way out, but then she died. Then it became my way out." I shrugged. "I don't know Mr. Hardin anymore than a stranger, and I'm not sure I want to marry an old man."

"Look, I don't really care a continental about your past or who you are, honey. I'm responsible for a cattle drive. My only concern is gettin' all the animals to Kansas. That's it."

"What if I don't want to marry Mr. Hardin?"

"That's your issue, not mine."

I had opened the door for him, hoping he would offer for me. Not having had a great deal of experience with men, I wondered if I had erred. Silence reined for a long and awkward moment, until I scrambled to my feet, putting on a brave face.

"I've got to help Marty. He's probably wondering where I am."

"You go do that."

I hated the stern expression, the dour look in his eyes. He had obviously woken on the wrong side of the bedroll. I had misjudged him completely or had I? An idea struck, propelling me to say, "I'll see if there's coffee. I'm sure Scott will want some. He was awfully drunk last night. He likes his eggs coddled." Wyatt's scowl deepened. "It's a pleasure to cook for a man who is so…appreciative." With that, I threw back my shoulders and stalked towards camp.

Ten

I realized I had made some mistakes. The first was meeting Eugenia Parker or whatever she said her name was. The second had been nearly giving into the urge to kiss her. The men had returned in the nick of time before I had crossed the line. Yet knowing these particulars changed absolutely nothing regarding the irritating and confusing position I had found myself in. Eugenia was like a magnet, constantly drawing me in.

I vowed to get her off my mind, spending the next night across camp far from her, while she had settled her bedroll near Scott Fallen. That young man had become far too attentive to her, which only increased my annoyance.

The days were long and hot, the animals having to be shepherded for miles at a time, the cowboys flanking the herd, with two in the rear to catch the stragglers. When I was on the move, it offered a respite from my troubling thoughts, but, as we settled in for the midday siesta, it vexed me greatly to find Eugenia in Scott's company, the two of them having developed a rapport.

A few days later, I came upon her wearing a pair of denim trousers. I stopped in my tracks, the bottom of my boots skidding on rocks. "What in tarnation is going on?"

She smiled brightly. "I borrowed them from Scott." She turned, giving me a view of her bottom, which set my mouth into a grim line. "They fit like a second skin, don't they?"

Son of a gun!

"I don't know why I never thought to wear men's pants. They're far more practical than a cumbersome dress. Don't you think?"

She had tied a length of rope around her tiny waist. The pants flared over her hips, the fit loose, but not loose enough to hide the sweet curve of her bottom. Hadn't she been distracting enough already? A tan blouse had been tucked in, the sleeves rolled up to the elbows. Although she was fully clothed, everything she wore clung to her, exposing an abundance of feminine curves.

"You're not happy." She smiled sympathetically. "Scott says I look lovely wearing his clothes."

"I just bet," I grated, brushing past her. "I gotta check on somethin'." I had the impression she enjoyed this game—goading me with that innocent smile, while teasing me with a body that tread a fine line towards sin. I stalked towards camp, scowling.

"Hey, boss," said Shep. "You get a load of Miss Parker?"

"I did."

"I gotta say, she sure fills 'em pants out."

I knelt by the fire, reaching for a metal kettle that I held with a cloth, as to not burn myself. Pouring a steaming cup of coffee, I settled in next to Shep, squinting under the sun. Men were sleeping, and most had found the shade of trees, while others had crawled under the chuckwagon. We would leave in an hour, but the animals needed to graze to keep their weight up.

"I'm not sure I'm gonna survive this," I murmured. He chuckled, and I assumed he knew what I was referring to. "She's not who she says she is."

"What do you mean?"

"She's not Sofia Parker. She said her name was Madsen or somethin'. She was Sofia's roommate. Mr. Hardin's fiancé died the night before she was due to leave."

"You don't say."

"She's a fraud."

"Did she say why? There has to be a reason."

"Somethin' about finding a way out."

He nodded pragmatically. "I can see that. Without a husband or family, it's hard goin' for a woman. She's just taking care of herself. Marryin' a rich old man isn't a half bad idea."

"She's a liar."

"She told you the truth, Wyatt. How does that make her a liar?"

I took a sip of coffee. "Most women have ulterior motives."

"She's lookin' for protection. If you had a sister, wouldn't you want her to marry well and have a good life?"

"I don't have sisters."

"I know that." His look was questioning. "Why can't you cut her some slack? We all know you're sweet on her. She's not the one Hardin's expectin'. He might not marry her now. That leaves the door open for you."

"For Scott, you mean."

"Aw…Scott's a harmless flirt. She don't look at him the way she looks at you. You're ten times the worth of that man anyhow. She knows that."

I never should have broached this subject. "I'm not lookin' for a wife, Shep. My lifestyle's not ideal for domestic tranquility. I prefer whiskey and harlots. They're easy and uncomplicated. Romantic entanglements are for fools."

"Well, if you let this one go, you might regret it. Some women are worth whatever aggravation they bring. Nobody's perfect, Wyatt. Everybody has flaws. But a pretty face and a kind heart are rare. Most women who look like that are full of themselves and they've perfected the art of lyin'."

"She did lie! She's here under a lie." Angered, I got to my feet. "I got horses to check. We're outta here soon."

"Yes, boss."

I stalked off, even more peeved than I was before. Why didn't any of my men see things the way I did? What in the blazes was wrong with them? The sound of gunfire caught my attention, as I reached for my revolver. Nelson ran towards me.

"What's that?"

"It's just practice! Scott's showin' Eugenia how to shoot. They're up around the bend in the canyon."

My mouth fell open. "Come again?"

"He's showin' her how to shoot."

"This I gotta see."

Another blast echoed, followed by another. With Nelson at my heels, we hurried towards the sound, winding our way through an old path that led downwards towards a flattened base of tallgrass. Eugenia and Scott stood off at a distance, he behind her, helping her aim the weapon, while she shot. I did not need to come any closer to see them, my anger having reached a boiling point.

Nelson was behind me. "See. They're hittin' old jugs."

Another shot rang out, while a jug fell back. "That they are."

"She's pretty good."

"He's pawing all over her."

"Well…I suppose." Nelson grinned. "He was always the helpful sort."

Disgusted, I turned away, as another shot echoed. "I got things to do. I can't stand around all day. We're leavin' soon. Gotta round up the cattle."

"Yes, boss."

After the boys had stirred from their naps, we were on the way again. I traveled with Shep, while the others were further ahead. The heat of the sun burned into my shoulders, as sweat trickled down my chest. It was exceptionally hot today, the summer being at its height along with a fair amount of humidity. We had a few more weeks of traveling before reaching Abilene, but, so far, we had made good time.

That evening, as we sat around the fire, I drank strong tea, while watching Eugenia and Scott, as they jabbered on incessantly. A spark of lightning flashed in the distance, and I worried that a storm was approaching. We had been lucky with the weather, but I knew it wouldn't hold out, and, as the evening wore on, the wind began to pick up. It was clear we were in for a long night.

We were mounted even before the rain began, the boys knowing full well the dangers of a stampede. The cows were liable to be spooked by the lightning. The gale was nearly upon us, the wind tossing bedrolls into the air, while pots on the chuckwagon had fallen to the ground. Eugenia and Marty scrambled to tie everything down, while the drovers near the head of the herd shepherded the animals to the right, forcing them to turn into a circle. The stragglers were brought in and encouraged to enter, while a tighter circle formed. This calmed the animals to an extent, but the effort was exhausting.

By the time we had returned to camp, a torrential downpour wet everything through, leaving the fire a smoking pit of ash. Water poured off the brim of my hat, soaking my arms. Everyone was thoroughly drenched and miserable. Marty and Eugenia had crawled into the chuckwagon, huddling together for warmth, while several men sought refuge beneath the supply wagon. Grasping a bedroll, I held the canvas over my head, while seated on a crate. I would try to wait out the weather and then go to sleep, but we would all suffer in the process.

In the morning, I didn't wake anyone, as none

of us had gotten much shuteye. My shirt and trousers were damp and water had collected in my boots, soaking my feet. Once the sun finally burned through the clouds, the men began to hang their things over tree limbs and rocks to facilitate the drying process. Several were naked from the waist up, walking through camp in bare feet.

A strange malaise had come over me, which I could not explain with any certainty. While sipping coffee by the fire, I hated having to watch Eugenia and Scott. They were thick as thieves, and, even though everyone had spent a dreadful night, she seemed lively and fresh, her glossy black hair hanging down her back. Those denim pants clung to her curves, while a pair of boots, men's boots, went nearly to her knees. Scott had donated more of his apparel; that much was obvious. They wandered off together again, and, a short while later, gunfire rang out.

"She'll be a sharpshooter before this is all over," said Shep, who sat next to me, crossing his legs before him.

I glared at him, feeling as sore as I looked. "Don't care."

He chuckled, but wisely dropped the topic. "When we leavin'?"

"Soon. Got a river to cross today. The rain will make things interesting."

He groaned. "Forgot about that. It could get

dicey."

"It *will* get dicey. It'll be a miracle, if the blasted cows don't drown. I'm not looking forward to it."

"I hear you."

"River crossings are dangerous on their own, but with this much rain…" I shrugged, "it's suicidal."

"Maybe we should wait a day."

"Can't. Gotta stick to the schedule." Another shot rang out, followed by several more.

"What do you want me to do?"

"Make sure everything's tied down. We gotta gather the calves."

"Yes, boss." He got to his feet. "Can't wait till Rawlins. I'm in dire need of a drink."

I nodded. "Me too." With little sleep and exhaustion, today was going to be grueling. I could feel it in my bones.

Eleven

I had made up my mind about a few things. While Wyatt ignored me and pretended he didn't care whether I breathed or died, I had struck up a friendship with Scott Fallen, finding him handsome enough and pleasant company. A life-changing revelation had been the moment I had pulled on a pair of denim slacks, finding the freedom and convenience astounding. Not only that, but I wore boots now too, real, honest to God cowboy boots, although they were a size too big.

Scott had given me a holster, which I wore with a belt. A revolver was now within easy reach. I had never felt this free before and capable of taking care of myself. I had been practicing shooting for days, hitting targets with increasing accuracy. I wanted to learn how to ride a horse and rope a steer, and I waited patiently for the lessons to begin, but first we had a daunting river to cross, the banks flooded, as the rain had been substantial.

I wore my hair in a low ponytail, while a wide-brimmed hat sat upon my head, the bonnets having been stashed deep inside a traveling bag. From the scowl on Wyatt's face whenever he saw me, I knew my appearance rankled him, but this only spurred me on further, adding an extra spring to my step. Scott had made it clear how attractive he found me in the figure-hugging pants. I could imagine the same response from Wyatt, although he strove to deny it.

He was the only man I had ever wanted to kiss. I was disappointed that he had not followed through with his promise, reliving that moment over and over again, while butterflies danced in my belly at the thought. Every female instinct I possessed told me that he fancied me, but, for some reason, he was determined to hate me, barely speaking to me and sleeping clear across camp from my bedroll at night. I had come to the conclusion that men were confusing and I did not understand them one bit.

Wyatt was saddling his horse, lacing the end of the latigo through the cinch ring. "Where do you want me?" I had surprised him, as he jerked slightly.

"Pardon?"

"Today. Do I travel with Marty or how are we gonna do this?"

His eyes roamed over my face. "Ride with Marty."

"All right." He continued to work on the saddle, double checking the cinch. "What will you do?"

"Bring the cattle across. It's gonna be a long day. They're not all that fond of wading through rushing water."

"It's dangerous, isn't it?"

"Of course." His look skirted on the edge of hostile.

"May I ask you something?"

"What?"

"Why are you angry with me? Did I say something or do something I shouldn't have? Are you mad that I'm not Sofia Parker? I'm sorry I lied; I truly am."

"Look, you do whatever you want to, honey. It's none of my business. If I gave you the impression that I…er…fancied you or somethin', then I apologize."

My heart sank, as disappointment registered. "I prefer you to any man I've ever met." I had laid all my cards on the table. "Maybe I like self-punishment, because whatever I'm feeling isn't reciprocated." I swallowed the lump in my throat. "How silly of me. I could've sworn you wanted me."

"You just don't know men. It's best you don't investigate things further. You'll be married once you reach Abilene. You'll look back on this as youthful folly."

He moved past me, but I grabbed his arm. "I just…" I wanted to beg him to reconsider, but my pride wouldn't let me. "I wish we could be friends." His stark look squashed that idea in its tracks.

"We gotta get a wiggle on. Time's a wastin'."

"Ouf, men!" I muttered, but he didn't hear me, as he had taken his horse away. "Fine. Be that way."

An hour later, we were on the road, the long line of cattle trudging along, while Marty and I blazed a path forward. Marty was unusually talkative today. "This has the potential for disaster. If I lose one pot, I'm gonna be steamed."

"We won't."

"It don't matter how many ways you secure somethin'; the river has a mind of its own. I've seen wagons, horses, cows, and people swept away. It ain't a pretty picture."

"I wonder how deep it is?"

"We're gonna find out soon enough. We'll be the first ones there."

"Do we wait for the others?"

"It's best, unless it's shallow and safe, but I

doubt it."

"I'm worried now."

He glanced at me. "You should be."

I placed my hand over his. "I'm not prone to praying, but I could say one for us, if you wanted me to."

"You go to church?"

"I always wanted to, but my ma hated it. Being what she was, she wasn't always welcome in places of worship."

"You're a good girl, Eugenia."

That was surprising. "Why do you say that?"

"You're kind and givin' and anything but a harlot."

I giggled, "I guess I should say thank you."

"You're a lively spirit and pleasant to be with. I thought you'd grate on my nerves with senseless prattle, but you're nice and quiet most days."

"I've had a lot to think about."

"I get my best thinkin' done on the trail."

I glanced off into the distance. "It sure is pretty here. Every day it looks different. Just when I get tired of grassland, I get desert; then, when I long for somethin' green again, here comes the prairie with wildflowers. Then there's the occasional prickly pear and yucca, just to keep me entertained."

"If you want to say a prayer on our behalf, then do it. You reminded me of some things just then. We should've tried to have a small Sunday service out here, but I doubt anyone brought a Bible."

"Maybe we can arrange something this Sunday."

"I think I'll leave it to you to organize."

Now I was nervous. The idea of firing a gun or riding a horse was easy compared to trying to remember Bible lessons, as my mind drew a blank on the topic. "I hope Scott went to church. I'm gonna need his help." Marty chuckled at that. "Okay, here goes my river prayer. God, please watch over us today and help us to make it across a big, horrible river without drowning or losing all our supplies. Thank you and amen."

He nodded, saying, "Nicely done. I feel better already."

The only time I could remember praying was the night a man with a gun attacked my mother at the brothel. I was sure he was going to kill her. I had hid in a closet, praying that God would protect her. In the end, he had put the weapon down, being subdued by several women, who waited for the sheriff to apprehend him. I had known girls who had been slain by clients, as they had gotten far too involved with them and domestic disputes had arisen. If it wasn't disease or drink or opium, it was a jealous lover or a murderous thug who ended the life of a prostitute. The lucky ones married, leaving the job behind, but most died far too young, as my mother had.

It was well past noon when Marty and I arrived at the river, finding the banks swollen, the water more than four to five feet high. We stood by the chuckwagon, observing the current that rushed past. Drifting logs and trees, which had been torn from the banks, were carried by the eddying tide, tossed around like toothpicks. Stunned, I could only gaze upon the obstacle in our path, fearful now of how we would manage the crossing.

Marty removed his hat, running fingers through his hair. "God save us."

"Isn't there a better spot to go over?" He shook his head. "It's too dangerous."

"You sit tight. I'm gonna see where the boys are." He patted my back. "We're gonna be fine, honey. I've seen worse."

I spent the time testing knots that secured the crates inside the chuckwagon. I stuffed cans into wooden boxes, while nailing the lids shut. By the time Marty returned, the other men appeared, bringing with them the first of the animals. The supply wagon that held the calves drew up behind us, and one of the boys, Martin, jumped down from the perch.

"Lordy. That's some river."

Wyatt approached, his expression sober. "You go on by yourself, Marty. That wagon don't need to be any heavier than it is."

"Yes, boss."

This announcement was a relief, as I had dreaded having to cross in the rickety conveyance. Marty disappeared around the other side, stepping up onto the wooden bench, while grasping the reins. His oxen, all six, were encouraged to go forward. While he trundled towards the water's edge, I gazed at Wyatt, who stood with his hands on his hips. Other men loitered, all on horseback.

"Will he be all right?"

"He should be."

The wagon rolled into the water, the rushing tide swallowing the wheels nearly to their tops. Marty shouted to the animals, cracking the whip on their rumps to urge them to hasten their movements. The wagon creaked and shook, the pots clanging, while I prayed he crossed in one piece. The bed had flooded with water; some items began falling out, drifting swiftly downstream and disappearing around the bend. While the animals struggled to gain a footing, working tirelessly to drag the heavy, water-laden burden to the other side, Marty continued to shout, snapping the whip freely. Once he had reached the opposite bank, the hind wheels emerging, I knew he had succeeded.

I clapped my hands together, yelling, "Good work, Marty!" I smiled at Wyatt, who continued to observe the events with a concerned, yet detached air. "How will I get across?"

"I'll take you." With that said, he grabbed my arm, bringing me to his horse. "Put your foot in the stirrup."

Never having been on a horse before, I felt a moment of fear. "Will he bite?"

"No, she won't bite, now up with you."

I flung a leg over, sitting comfortably in the saddle. "Oh, my." I touched the animal, feeling the coarse mane. She did not seem to mind that someone other than Wyatt had mounted her. To my astonishment, he got on behind me, his arm going around my waist, drawing me close.

"You hang on. We'll be over in seconds."

His warm breath near my ear made me shiver with pinpricks of pleasure. "I can't wait to learn how to ride one of these."

"Hang on."

He spurred the horse towards the water, its legs submerging within moments, wetting us to the thigh. My boots would be soaked, but it was the only way to cross safely. The current pushed against us, the strength of the water a force to be reckoned with, but we weren't trapped for long, the horse easily traversing to the other side, its body undulating beneath me. Wyatt's arm hadn't left my waist, holding me securely. I glanced at him over my shoulder, but I had been too close and our hats collided, mine falling to the ground.

"That was exciting." I was drenched nearly to the waist, but it had been a thrill. "I want to do the next river alone, with my own horse." I wrapped my arms around his neck, hugging him. "Thank you, Wyatt."

He pushed me away, grumbling, "Go on, and get down now. I've work to do."

Twelve

It was a form of torture being trapped with a woman like Eugenia. I had tried my darnedest to deny my feelings and pretend they weren't there, but it was impossible. After the river crossing, we stopped on the outskirts of Rawlins; the boys were chomping at the bit to get to town and have a drink, while I was in a different form of agony altogether. I knew I was weakening, my resolve crumbling. I was dangerously close to giving into acting upon the way I felt. Perhaps, a night of liquor and women was just what I needed to get my mind off things.

Eugenia had learned to ride, having been taught by an obsequious and attentive Scott Fallen, who I had grown to hate with a passion reserved only for men who had crossed me in my lifetime. I was left to ponder the depth of this anger, while finishing a plateful of stew, which I had dunked several biscuits into. I was more than ready to cut loose with the boys tonight; the atmosphere around camp was jovial and light, although some tensions had simmered over the last few days. The natives were restless, needing to blow off steam.

By the time we had saddled up, I tipped my hat to Marty. "See you later."

He had wanted to stay with Eugenia, to watch over her, which absolved me of all obligations where she was concerned. I could raise heck with the best of them tonight and not crawl back to camp until dawn, which was exactly what I planned to do.

"You bring me back a bottle."

"You know spirits aren't allowed on the trail."

"Aw, please, don't make me beg." He smiled contritely. "You're off havin' a wild time, while I'm stuck minding the youngster."

"You don't have to do that," said Eugenia. "I'm perfectly capable of taking care of myself."

She stood with her hands on her hips, inadvertently thrusting out her breasts, which were hidden by a thin chemise and an even thinner blouse. I did not want to look at her, hating how my body responded and cursing the day I ever met her.

"It's up to you, Marty. We're only about a mile away. You should come with us for a spell."

"Well…"

"I'll be fine." Eugenia flung her hair over a shoulder in a purely feminine manner. "I can keep the fire going and watch over things." Scott had given her a Bible, and she had been reading it, although she needed assistance in understanding some of the words. Mr. Fallen was always on hand in these instances.

"Maybe I'll stay with you," said Scott, who had joined us.

"You should enjoy yourself too. You don't have to worry about me. I'm completely at ease with this now. I was scared the first time, but I know how to shoot. I can hit my target. I'll be just fine."

Disgusted by the sweet smile she bestowed upon Scott, I turned away, encouraging the horse forward. "I'm off. You do what you want." There was a barstool in a saloon with my name on it. I planned to get my fill tonight, and there would be no one to stop me. And I would not hesitate to take the first whore I saw either, needing desperately to find relief from weeks of pent-up frustration that had been brewing inside of me.

With this in mind, I spurred the horse to a gallop, with Shep and Nelson coming up quick; the boys and I were of the same mind. Rawlins was tiny and desolate, but the main thoroughfare teamed with wagons and men, other cowboys having come in from another trail. We tied our horses to the hitching post, as anticipation had my mouth watering at the prospect of smooth whiskey. I would be plenty upset if the proprietors cut their good whiskey, as that would only give me a bellyache. The brothel was lit up like a Christmas tree, every window blazed with light. A silhouette of a couple engaged in an intimate encounter caught my eye.

Shep noticed too. "That's what I'll be doin' in two hours, boys."

I chuckled, "Amen to that."

Several of the junior cowboys arrived, tipping their hats in our direction, while securing their animals. I had taken to the steps, eager to find a place at the bar. Shep and Nelson followed me in, where conversations stopped, while men eyed us. It was a mutual assessment, and, when we were deemed harmless, all activities resumed, including the piano music.

"Whiskey," I said, and a glass came my way. The bartender poured a shot. "Thank you." I downed it in one swallow, setting the glass on the counter. "More."

Shep and Nelson joined me, sitting on either side, as an aggressive drinking session commenced. I eyed the customers through the mirrored wall, spying two of my boys chatting up the saloon girls. One of the ladies stood on a chair and sang *Baldy*

Green, while men stomped their feet and tapped the tables with their six-shooters. The joviality of the patrons helped to melt away my dour mood, leaving me more relaxed than I could last remember. After the third or fourth drink, I had begun to buzz from the inside out. Shep had left to join a card game, while Marty approached.

"So, you did decide to come after all."

"Eugenia assured me she was fine, so," he shrugged, "I reckon I'm free for a while. I'll have a couple and head back."

"That girl knows how to take care of herself."

"Bein' this close to town, I'm concerned about rustlers, Wyatt. There's more than one group of cowboys here."

"I thought of that."

"It's why I'm headin' back."

"I got some business to take care of in the parlour house before I even entertain the notion of returning to camp."

"I hope you work out your issues, boss." He nodded knowingly. "I can see the tension in your face. You've had a rather nasty chip on your shoulder too. For your sake, I hope you find…ahem…relief."

"Your concern over my well-being is thoughtful, Marty. It really is, but unnecessary."

"I hate to see a man suffer. That's all."

I pushed away from the bar, throwing coins on

the counter. "Well, on that note, I think I'm gonna see if the grass is greener on the other side of the street."

"Good luck."

I placed the hat on my head. "I'll be back when I'm done."

He chuckled at that.

Shep and Nelson were otherwise occupied; the noise level in the saloon had risen, as the occupants had grown more intoxicated. Laughing and shouting could be heard all the way into the thoroughfare. A fight was in progress as well, which was typical. Someone was getting the tar beat out of them, but I paid it no mind, as none of the combatants were my boys. Striding towards the two-story clapboard sided house, I entered a familiar environment, of velvet sofas, polished furniture, and the aroma of tobacco, which was mixed with heavy perfume.

I wasn't at all particular tonight, approaching a painted harlot in a pink and black dress. "I need a woman. Don't care what she looks like, as long as she's enthusiastic."

"Well, hello, handsome." She ran a chubby hand over my shoulder. "I think I've got the perfect girl for you. Melinda's a natural redhead, but it'll cost you."

There were rumors that redheads were wild and fearless in bed, but I had not proven that theory yet. "I guess that sounds like somethin' I might be interested in."

"Of course you are. I'll see if she's available, cowboy." She winked at me.

"Please."

I waited, while men drank and chatted with the soiled doves. Some were led to the stairs and out of sight. The haven that waited on the second floor was a myriad of bedrooms, which would see quite a few customers this evening. The woman I had spoken to approached, bringing with her a surprisingly fresh-faced redhead, who wore a silk robe.

"Here she is. Melinda's ready for you, cowboy."

I nodded. "Thank you." She left us then, sauntering off to someone who had just arrived. I stared at the woman before me, finding her more than acceptable for my needs. "Wyatt." I held out my hand, which she shook.

"Would you like a drink, sir?"

"No, I'm good."

"Shall we go upstairs then?"

"Sounds like a plan."

"Follow me." As she walked, she asked, "What brings you to these parts?"

"Cattle." I wasn't in the mood for small talk, admiring the way her hips swayed, as she took to the steps.

"Oh, we see a lot of fellas from the cattle trade come through here." We were on the landing, which was dimly illuminated, the sounds of laughter and talking drifting up from the parlor. "You sure are handsome, Wyatt. It's a nice change from all the curly wolves I've seen." She reached for a door, opening it. "We get some rough sorts through here, and, frankly, they don't smell all that nice." I had followed her, noting the tidy room, the lamp turned down low, and a single bed with a dark blue quilt. As she pivoted to face me, I grabbed her. "Oh!" I slid my hand into the silken robe, while I took the liberty of feeling her intimately. "My goodness." Undoing my belt, I left the gun and holster on a nearby table, dropping my pants, which fell to my ankles. Her gaze lowered. "You sure are in fine form, mister."

Talking wasn't necessary, as I turned her from me, shoving the material of the robe aside, while seeking the relief I so desperately wanted. Her hands dropped to the bed, as she braced for the onslaught. Female murmurings of pleasure, which were more theatrical than real, filled the room. I hadn't been with a woman in quite some time, and I gave her no quarter, using her roughly. To my chagrin, an image flashed in my mind of an exotically beautiful woman with dark, expressive eyes.

As I found the release I so urgently sought, my

body expelling a rush of physical and emotional energy, I blurted, "Eugenia!" I then collapsed upon the prostitute, landing on the bed, which creaked from the weight.

She turned to look at me, but it wasn't the face I wanted to see. "You sure were energetic, sir. We can go again in a few minutes, if you want to."

I stared at the ceiling, noting a series of water spots. "Yeah, probably." It was going to be a long night, and one that I was prepared to pay dearly for, as these services would not come cheap. I could not think of any other way to get Eugenia out of my mind. She did not belong there, but she had taken occupancy like an unwanted houseguest who refused to budge. "It'll be better by mornin'," I muttered to myself.

"I sure hope so, or I'll have to call in reinforcements. I might have to anyway."

My pants were still around my ankles. I kicked them free. "Give me your best shot."

Bawdy laughter filled the room.

Thirteen

I wasn't scared this time, sitting by the fire and watching the flames, while the sound of crickets resonated around me. There was enough light to read by, and I had been enjoying bits and pieces of the Bible, mostly those passages I could understand. My schooling was lacking, because my mother had never seen to it, but I had learned to read from one of the prostitutes at the brothel.

When my eyelids became heavy, I slid beneath the covers on the bedroll and turned to my side, yawning. I was asleep within minutes, but something woke me a while later. Confused, I turned to find Wyatt, who had joined me on the bedroll. He smelled heavily of whiskey. Stunned, I did not know what to expect from this surprising, yet wonderful, turn of events. He drew me into his arms, holding me so close I could barely breathe.

His lips grazed my forehead, but he kept his mouth on my skin, while his arms crushed me.

"I don't think it worked," he murmured.

"What worked?"

"There is no cure. I'm just gonna have to live with it."

I had no idea what he was talking about, but the closeness lifted my spirits greatly. He had been one of the first to return; even Marty, who said he would only have a drink or two, was nowhere to be seen. Enjoying every moment of Wyatt's weakness, as he was horribly intoxicated, I sighed blissfully, relaxing in his arms, my eyes closing.

By morning, I found myself alone, which was disappointing. As the camp began to come alive, several cowboys were ill, vomiting into the bushes nearby, while others nursed headaches, moaning and muttering under their breaths. There were bags and dark circles beneath eyes, because none of those boys had gotten a sound sleep. A few were still in town, because horses were missing. Marty had opened the back of the chuckwagon, chopping meat and onions for a hearty morning meal. Not knowing where Wyatt had gone, I slid my boots on and headed for the creek, wanting to wash up. On the way there, I spotted a man on the ground, which gave me a shock.

"Mister?" I realized it was one of the cowboys, who had collapsed from drink and slept where he lay. "Oh, goodness. That must've been some party."

At the creek, I dunked my hands into cold water, washing my face and teeth. I had slept beautifully; most of the night had been a dream, being in Wyatt's arms. He had come back for me, and this thought left me elated. It was my wish to be with him, but he was stubbornly refusing to admit he wanted me. On the way back to camp, the sleeping cowboy had disappeared, and I found him near the fire, sitting on a crate, while holding his face in his hands.

"I'm never drinkin' again," he muttered. Laughter followed this announcement.

Wyatt appeared moments later, looking the worse for wear. He held a tin cup, sipping the brew gingerly. He kept his gaze low, finding the fire fascinating. Had he forgotten everything? I would not allow myself to feel despondent over this, because I had been safe in his arms for hours. That should have been enough to satisfy me…but it wasn't.

Once everyone had been fed and things had been put away, we began the day, just like all the others, Marty and I traveling ahead, while the men followed, the line of cattle stretching out behind us. At lunch, the boys were still nursing headaches and illness; the effects of having too much liquor was slow to wear off. By evening, most were nearly recovered, some laughing about their adventures, while others realized they had spent their wages for a month. Wyatt was strangely quiet, and, later that night, he slept across camp from me. I unhappily accepted the fact that he had no memory of being on my bedroll.

The days began to wear on in a pattern that had been established from the beginning. Marty and I had perfected the mealtimes, and I had learned a thing or two about cooking, especially when the supplies began to run low. We tossed every cut of beef imaginable into the "son-of-a-gun-stew". The stomach, liver, heart, kidneys, and tongues were all edible, everything except the hair and horns. It was surprisingly delicious, and the cowboys had no qualms about eating cow brains, as they thickened the concoction, especially after being mixed with flour.

From Oklahoma, we crossed into Kansas; a sense of expectancy abounded, because the journey was nearing a close. I had thought a great deal about my future, worrying that I would now be forced to marry a rich old man, who was a stranger. I had hoped Wyatt would offer for me, but he had kept his distance. At times, it was as if he went out of his way to avoid me. Scott, although attentive and sweet, remained a friend. He was heading east after this run, wanting to see his family again. I had enjoyed his company and all the things he had taught me about riding and shooting. Roping cattle had been my failing, as I never was able to toss the rope far or high enough.

On the last night, near the outskirts of Abilene, Marty and I ambled on ahead of the boys, looking for a spot to make camp. He called to the oxen, encouraging them forward.

"We should make somethin' special tonight," he said.

"Fruit pie. We've canned cherries."

"I thought they'd run out?"

"I found a few in the bottom of a crate yesterday."

He smiled, the edges of his eyes crinkling. "The boys will like that."

"They like anything sweet."

His arm went around my shoulder. "Just like you."

"Aw…stop that."

"I never traveled with a woman before. I was always a lone wolf. You've been surprisingly good company, Eugenia, and I'm gonna miss you when you're gone."

"You've been like the pa I never had."

"You're like the daughter I never had, or maybe I did." His grin was wicked. "I probably fathered a kid or two…somewhere."

"I didn't think I would like this. What an adventure."

"You did good. Real good. You got a whole new bag of skills now. You can cook and shoot and ride. You'd make some farmer an excellent wife. You're already trained for the position."

I giggled at that. "It sounds like I should take out an ad in the paper."

"You won't need to do that. You're marryin' Mr. Hardin. He'll keep you in fine style, Eugenia. You'll want for nothin'."

"Is he a kind man? I worry about that. I…what if I hate his looks?"

"He's older and fatter, but from what I remember, he seemed like a good man. I've met him twice. He's an astute businessman; that's for certain."

"I heard he's had two wives."

"They died. The first died young, the second, I don't know." He shrugged. "Longevity isn't a given."

I thought of my mother and Sofia. "I know."

We had stopped near a line of trees. "I'm gonna get a fire goin'. If we're makin' pies, we gotta hop to it."

"All right."

Once the men appeared, dusty and exhausted from a long day in the saddle, the camp was ready, bedrolls had been laid out, and a roaring fire held two Dutch ovens with pies and biscuits baking inside. The aroma lingered, along with Marty's salt pork and potato stew, which was infused with fried onions for flavor. The conversations were peppered with plans and ideas for future endeavors and what the boys would spend their money on.

I'd had a slice of cherry pie, savoring each bite. The men groaned their appreciation, while eating, nodding in my direction. "Nice work, Eugenia."

"Thank you."

After having licked the plate clean, my face was sticky. Making my way to a nearby stream, I took a moment to gaze at the surroundings, not fearing the dark in the least. The moon hung brightly overhead, illuminating a small path. I knew immediately that I wasn't alone, because a man sat on a rock a distance off. It was Wyatt. This was possibly the last time he and I would share the same space together. There were so many things I had wanted to say to him, but I had not been able to. He had sent out mixed signals from the start, yet my female intuition knew he was enamored of me, although he would never admit it.

I bent to wash, rinsing my face, while he stared my way. "Did you have pie?" I asked.

"I did. It was really good."

"I'm glad you liked it." I approached him. "Why are you hiding out here?"

"Just thinkin'."

"It's almost over."

"Yeah."

"What will you do?"

"I'll work for Peter Whitmore next. I'm bringin' his cattle west."

"You won't even rest for a spell?"

"I can rest when I'm dead."

"Wyatt?"

"Yeah?"

"Oh…never mind." His attitude bothered me, and I tried not to let it show, but it was difficult.

"What is it? You wanna say somethin', so say it."

I met his gaze, feeling wetness prick the backs of my eyes. "I adore you."

"I'm aware of that. You got that soft look in your eyes. I think you're seein' way too much in me, honey."

It pained me to hear those words. I had so little experience with men. It was possible that most of them behaved like Wyatt, and I had fallen prey far too easily. Perhaps, I could have protected myself, had I known the dangers of attraction. "So, there's no chance for us?"

"I don't think so. You'd do better with Hardin."

"How so?"

"He'll take good care of you."

"How do you know?"

"He's rich."

Anger suddenly prickled. "And that's enough

for a happy marriage? You think that's all I want? Some rich old man?"

"Don't most women?"

"You lousy…stupid cowboy!" I wanted to use stronger words, but for propriety's sake, I had held back. "I might be green about men, but I know you want me."

"I'd want any hot-blooded woman. I'm a man."

I blinked away tears, hating that I had fallen so hard for someone who wasn't worth my spit. "I see now."

His look softened. "Honey, I'm tryin to save you from a world of hurt. You don't wanna get tangled up with me. I can't be in one place for too long. I stir up trouble wherever I go, and it's not somethin' I want to expose other people to."

"Aren't you too old to be behaving that way?" He had been entirely composed and responsible on this cattle drive. I had to wonder, if he was painting himself in a poor light, so I would feel grateful that he hadn't offered for me.

A crooked grin lifted the edges of his mouth. "I guess."

"I have something to say to you."

"Shoot."

"I think you're a liar and a thief. You lie when you say you don't have feelings for me, and you've stolen my heart. You promised me a kiss, and you never followed through on it. Even the worst scoundrels on earth can give a girl a kiss, but not you." I threw my shoulders back. "I hope you have a happy life, Wyatt. I would've married you, if you had asked." Tears flooded. "I just wish I hadn't fallen in love with you. I'll regret that for the rest of my life."

Fourteen

Her words burned a wound straight into my soul, feeling like the end of a sword that had been left in a fire. The sincerity in her voice and the anger and hurt in her eyes were my undoing. Every word she had said was the truth. She was about to walk away when I grabbed her, dragging her too me. A stunned gasp escaped her lips, which had fallen open in surprise. She had thrown down quite a challenge, and I would be damned, if I didn't pick it up. I held her face in my hands, intent on claiming those full, pink lips.

She knew what I planned, as her eyes widened. It was the look of surrender. I had seen it before on countless women, but it had never meant anything to me—until now. But I had known she was susceptible to me nearly since the beginning. This was the reason I had tried to stay away and why I fought with my instincts to deny the connection I felt. I had blamed my weakness on whiskey or the isolation and lack of women, but I knew that had nothing to do with it. It would be the same, even in a city with a million people. She would still be the only one...

I worried that once I had kissed her and tasted the promise of what she gave so freely, I would not be able to tear myself away. I'd profess my love and offer marriage, thereby committing myself forever. This was a real fear, but I forced it aside, as our lips met. Closing my eyes, I inhaled her scent, the sweet, natural musk of her skin, while her arms snaked around my neck and she pressed herself to me. I sat on a rock, which was nearly three feet off the ground, while she settled between my thighs.

"Oh, Wyatt," she breathed.

The sound of my name spoken in such a manner sent a sensual chill down my spine, propelling me to kiss her deeper, driving my tongue into her mouth, which she readily accepted. Her fingers were in my hair now, grasping me with increasing urgency. My hands weren't idle. They had pulled the blouse out from the denim pants, freeing the material. I explored her at my leisure, drifting over the contours of her belly, which trembled at my touch.

She leaned further, forcing me onto my back,

while her lips connected with my neck, where she kissed and nibbled at my skin. It was impossible to hide my arousal; the evidence had produced a rather sizable bulge in my trousers, which I hoped she did not notice. She had unbuttoned my shirt, exposing my chest, where she lavished dozens of kisses, even being so bold as to suckle a nipple. Her eagerness was a worry, because I was rapidly reaching the point of no return.

Most encounters with the ladies in a brothel were never this intimate, never this pleasurable. It was perfunctory copulation at best, and then, once the deed was done, I'd drop the money and run. They were not inclined to seduce me with their touch or kiss or sweet murmurings. There was no feeling, no attraction. That was why Eugenia was dangerous. She had pulled the shirt free, clawing away at my belt buckle, while kissing my belly, her tongue sliding into the indentation there. It had gone too far.

"Honey." I sat up, desperately trying to rouse myself from the lustful stupor, but wishing I didn't have to. "We gotta slow down."

Her arms went around my neck, while she leaned into me, murmuring, "Oh, Wyatt…oh…please don't say that. We only have tonight. I want you…to be my first…my only."

The heat of her breath was in my ear. The urgency in her tone matched my own, but, if I let things go further, nothing would ever be the same again. "Sweetheart, you're…" I made the mistake of looking at her, seeing those huge dark eyes glistening with emotion, her chest rising and falling with each breath. "I feel the same, Eugenia, but it's not right. I can't make love to you on a rock. You deserve so much more. You deserve a nice house and a comfortable bed and the security of a man who can take care of you and provide for your future."

She held my face. "You could do that."

"No, honey."

"I don't need fancy things. I've never had them. I'm happy with little, but I'd be happier if you were with me."

"I'll always be grateful I met you. Watchin' you has been frustrating and entertaining. You're a member of the trail crew now. You fit right in." I grinned. "But those pants on you are sinful."

"You make me cry, Wyatt. You're the only man I've ever wanted. How am I supposed to settle with someone else, when all I think about is you?"

I touched her face, wiping away a tear. I hated seeing a woman cry. "Life ain't easy. The choices are never the ones we really want, but we got to. You'd hate me, if we were together. I've some bad habits, and I'm ornery, especially if I'm in one place too long. I've gotten better over the years, cause the war messed with my head somethin' awful, but I don't think I'll ever be all right."

"What do you mean?"

"I…get flashes of things, images of killin' people. I killed lots of people. People who had families, children, wives—"

She put her finger over my lips. "That's war, Wyatt. It was a horrible war. At least you fought on the right side."

"There is no right or wrong, it was just hell, honey."

"I don't expect you to be perfect. I just want to be with you."

"I come from a family of outlaws. Everybody but my younger brother Charlie has done somethin' they weren't supposed to. You'd be tying yourself to a family like that. My mother is a remarkable woman, but she's a bit of a hell raiser herself."

She smiled. "I'd fit in perfectly. My mother was a prostitute. You think I'm perfect, but I'm not. Did you know I sometimes hid under the bed and went through a fella's billfold? I'd take a few extra dollars, and he'd be none the wiser."

"Is that so?"

"That's how ma and I made extra money. Money we didn't have to share with the house."

"I see."

"I was her partner in crime. I'm a thief too."

"Well, that would earn you a spot at the Carson dinner table, but it doesn't change things. I'm sorry. I don't want to offer you false hope. I can't make any promises, cause I'm liable to break 'em all. You're worth more than that."

Tears flooded her eyes. "Why must you be so stubborn? Can't we just give it a try? I adore you, you stupid man. I wish I didn't, but I do. All I do is think about you. How could I possibly be with someone else, when you're the only one I want?"

"You'll come to thank me in time."

She pushed against my chest. "No I won't. I'll pine for you, is what I'll do. You've already ruined me for any other man."

"That shows your inexperience. There are far better candidates out there, believe me. I'm damaged goods, Eugenia. I'm not worth the trouble."

"I disagree, but I can see nothing I say will change your mind." The warmth in her eyes had been replaced with anger. "I would've loved you until the day I died. I would've given you anything you wanted and more. We could've been happy, even living in a dugout. You won't even take a chance on us. You've given up before we even started."

"You're right." I nodded somberly, feeling gutted, but this was for the best.

The tears fell in earnest now, her mouth

quivering. "You're a fool, Wyatt Carson. I wish you the best of luck in your endeavors. I just hope I don't end up hating you for throwing me away like unwanted trash."

She turned, but those words could not be the last we said between us. My arms went around her, while my mouth was near her ear. "No, Eugenia. No. Let's not leave it like this. I know you're mad, and you have every right to be, but please know that I adore you, honey. If things were different, I'd get down on one knee. If I thought for one moment I was the right man for you, I'd ask you to marry me. I'm savin' you a world of hurt by lettin' you go. You can't see it right now, but I am."

"Can we be together tonight? I don't want to sleep alone."

The sleeping arrangement by the fire was hardly private, but this would prevent things from going too far. "All right." I was grateful our last night would not be wasted on anger. I did not want to say goodbye on those terms, although she would be plenty hurt in the morning when I left her in Abilene in the care of Isaac Hardin. I took her hand. "Look at me." She met my gaze. "Will you stop cryin'?" I wiped away a tear.

"I'll try, but I hurt, Wyatt. I can't help it. It feels like somebody ripped open a hole in my chest."

Her words cut through me, shredding

whatever control I had left. I wrapped my arms around her, holding her close, hating that things would end this way. In that warm and humid night, with the sound of crickets and trickling water, what should have been the realization of a dream was actually the death of one. I was about to let the only woman I had ever loved step out of my life.

We wandered back to camp to find most of the men sleeping, while the fire had dimmed. Marty and Shep were in conversation, while Nelson slept with his hat over his head. Eugenia and I settled on my bedroll, while several interested glances came our way. I drew her into my arms, my lips grazing her forehead, while I stared at the stars overhead. Her arm was across my belly, while one of her legs had gone over mine, in a possessive manner. Neither of us seemed inclined to talk, the emotions from earlier left to fester; the feeling was melancholy at best.

A rather large part of me knew I was making a mistake. If I let this woman walk out of my life—I would never see her again. She would marry Mr. Hardin and have his children, living in a rambling house in Abilene. I would not have to worry over her welfare or her happiness, as she would eventually find a measure of peace and even contentment in her new surroundings. She was a hardy girl and far stronger than she gave herself credit for. I had seen her blossom on the trail, from a timid wallflower to a range-riding cowgirl in denim pants. She was a survivor, and she would get on just fine without me.

But…would I be able to live without her? That question kept me up most of the night, and, as the morning sun began to peek out over the horizon, I knew the answer…and it wasn't pretty.

Fifteen

That last day on the trail was like living through a series of small deaths. I had spent the night with Wyatt, sleeping in his arms, while my dreams had been filled with morose and tearful goodbyes. He wasn't able to offer for me, although his reasons were flimsy at best. There seemed to be nothing I could say to him to change his mind. The future lay wide-open, but it did not include Wyatt Carson.

After the breakfast dishes had been washed and the Dutch oven scrubbed clean, Marty and I packed the chuckwagon one last time. By noon, we would be in Abilene. We had seen other drovers this morning, moving cows north, intent on bringing them to the railheads. We would follow them shortly.

Wyatt had left with Scott and Shep to round

up the stragglers and retrieve the calves. When he returned, our things were packed, and we were ready to depart. I sat on the wagon, while Marty yoked the oxen, preparing for the last stretch of ride. I didn't want to, but I could not help staring at Wyatt, admiring the way he sat his horse, his face shielded by the wide brim of his hat. I knew what it was like to be kissed by him and the memory left me in a constant state of craving. My face and neck were chafed from the roughness of his beard and my lips swollen, a reminder of the pleasure I had found in his arms.

I had worn a dress today, a violet creation with a fitted bodice, waist cinching corset, and a straw bonnet. I had not donned a corset in weeks, and the constriction made me want to cry. I had been entirely at ease in denim slacks and a blouse, wishing I did not have to return Scott's clothing.

My adventure was at an end; the time I had spent on the trail had been thrilling and unforgettable. I had learned how to shoot and ride and cook. I had slept with the men out in the open, with only the stars overhead to offer protection. I had fallen in love on this journey, but the bittersweet sting of rejection had hardened me, leaving me with twinges of resentment. This was not the ending I had been hoping for, but I had never known life to be merciful. Wishes and dreams were for those who were born under luckier stars. Good fortune happened to other people, not to someone who had been raised in a brothel, and whose father had never been named.

The final hour was the worst, seeing the outline of the town in the distance, but ambling towards it in slow motion, as if the chuckwagon was almost standing still. My future husband resided in Abilene, and, although I hadn't a clue if I would even marry him, I knew he waited. With every mile, a pit grew in my belly, filled with an empty yearning for something better, but, perhaps, I was asking for too much. I should be grateful that I had traveled in peace and safety and that I had arrived at my destination in good health. I should be grateful I hadn't died like Sofia or my mother. Life would be what I made out of it, and the sooner I resolved to put on a brave face, the better my chances of a good outcome.

"Well, girl," said Marty, squinting. "You've been a pleasant companion. I'll miss you."

I hugged him. "I'll miss you too."

"I know you're gonna go on and marry and have children. I wish you the best of luck."

"Thank you."

The railhead was on the other end of town, near the train station, where there were fences in place to hold all the cattle. It teemed with men, while the sounds and smells were nearly overpowering. Marty drew the wagon to the side, not having the means to go further, but we weren't needed anyhow. Wyatt and his boys began the arduous task of shepherding the animals into the facility, while I sat stoically watching. These animals would be processed and then sent on their way at the behest of their owner, Mr. Hardin.

The heat of the midday sun had left me slightly dizzy, as moisture beaded on my forehead. I yearned for a drink of water, and I left the wagon, striding towards a nearby building that was surrounded by a covered boardwalk. Men loitered outside, some entering and leaving through the double wooden doors. It was cooler within, as a fan circled the air above. The space appeared to be some sort of meeting room with chairs and tables arranged in the center. Several well-dressed gentlemen were in conversation; papers and maps had been laid out over a table. They turned to look at me.

"I'm sorry to interrupt. Is there water?"

A tall man in a gray and blue suit said, "Yes, ma'am. It's awful hot out there, isn't it?" He poured fluid from a pitcher into a glass. "Here you are."

"Thank you."

I had their attention, yet I tried to be as unobtrusive as possible, because I had interrupted a business meeting. While I drank, one of the men stared at me; he was older and grayer, yet distinguished. I had finished the water, leaving the glass on a table. Turning to go, a hand stopped me.

"I beg your pardon." It was the older man who had approached. "I'm Isaac Hardin. I'm expecting someone by the name of Sofia Parker. I noticed you came in with the Carson team, and I was wondering if you could tell me if Sofia traveled with you?"

Oh, my goodness. "I…I'm sorry, but Sofia passed away before she was able to leave." The truth had tumbled from my lips.

He blinked. "Passed away? What on earth happened?"

"I was her roommate in San Antonio. I tried to help her, but an infection ravaged her body. I have all the letters you sent her. That will prove that I knew her."

His countenance was grim. "I see."

"I…have to tell you something, sir. I told your men I was Sofia. I lied to secure passage here. I know you were expecting Sofia, but maybe…you might find me an acceptable bride instead."

His look was considering. "What's your name?"

"Eugenia Madsen. My mother was a prostitute, and I was raised in a brothel." I felt it was best to be truthful. If he found my past distasteful, he would turn away now. "I've not had much of an education, but I can read. Your boys taught me how to rope and ride and shoot." I couldn't help grinning at the memories. "It was the time of my life, sir."

Mr. Hardin," said a man who had approached. "We're ready to begin the inventory."

"I'll be there in a moment." He turned to me. "I'd like to talk to you later, Miss Madsen, if you don't mind. I can arrange for a room at the Drover's Cottage. I'd be delighted, if you would join me for dinner."

"Where's the hotel?" This request was stunning. I thought for certain he would reject me.

"I'll have my man take you there. He'll fetch you later as well."

"Thank you."

"Then we can discuss this situation in detail. I appreciate your honesty."

"I'm sorry about Sofia."

He ignored that. "And bring the letters as well. I'll need to see them."

"Yes, sir."

He nodded, taking his leave, while I watched him go. He was older than I had expected, but pleasant enough. I had learned to read people from an early age, and I did not sense anything untoward. Some men radiated hostility and negativity, my instincts warning me that they were dangerous. Mr. Hardin was none of those things, but I would have to reserve my judgment until I knew more of his character, and that would take time.

I had thought that I would see Wyatt again, that he would say goodbye to me, but it was not meant to be. Mr. Hardin had sent a carriage, and I had waved to Marty, as I had gotten in. He was the only one who witnessed my departure. It was strange that I had not been able to say goodbye to any of the boys I had come to know on the trail. With sadness in my heart, I was taken to the hotel and given a lovely room with a large window that opened onto the street. I should have been relieved to find myself in such agreeable surroundings, but my spirit felt crushed.

After resting and bathing, I changed into a blue skirt and fitted bodice, fixing my hair in a bun. I gazed at myself in a mirror, marveling at how my skin had darkened from the sun. The time I had spent traveling had altered my appearance, but, once I was indoors again, the color would fade. I tucked the letters into a small bag, and sat on the bed, waiting to be summoned. I swung booted feet back and forth, nervously anticipating the evening.

A knock on the door brought me to my feet. Mr. Hardin's servant had arrived to fetch me. I was escorted to the first floor and through to a bustling dining room, filled with ladies and gentlemen, while waiters came and went. I worried my dress was not smart enough, while anxious energy coursed through me. These emotions were hidden beneath a veneer of a bland, yet happy countenance. A table had been set towards the back with an ivory cloth and sparkling china. Candles had been lit as well. Mr. Hardin cut an elegant figure in a dark suit with a black top hat. He stood, as I arrived.

"Good evening, Miss Madsen."

"Hello." My chair was held out for me. "Thank you." After I was seated, the waiter placed a napkin on my lap.

"Would you care for some wine?"

"I would. Thank you." Reaching into the bag, I withdrew the letters. "Here is the correspondence."

He eyed the bundle dispassionately. "My man's done some checking. What you say is the truth."

"It is."

"You were a resident of the Fielding Boarding House. You worked as a washerwoman."

"I did."

"Your mother's name is Rita Regina Madsen. She passed away on April 23rd 1869 of a condition best described as an affliction of the lungs. She struggled to breathe, and this led to her death."

That was disconcerting. "You have been busy."

"I like to know what I'm getting myself involved in."

"I know nothing about you."

"We'll come to that in good time."

"Yes, sir." This conversation was businesslike and emotionally void.

A waiter came to take our order, and after he left, Mr. Hardin said, "I need to know the extent of your relationship with Mr. Wyatt Carson. There are rumors you were lovers."

Something flipped over in my belly at the mention of Wyatt's name. "No sir. I kissed him, but that's all."

"I see."

"Is there anything else you wish to know?"

"I'm sorry about this, but it must be done. Please forgive my crudeness, but…are you a virgin?"

I swallowed nervously. "Yes. I am."

He sat back in the chair, his expression stern. "I'll have to take you on your word. I would never force an exam on a woman."

"I feel like a cow you've just paid for." I had spoken my mind, but I wasn't finished. "I'm not perfect, Mr. Hardin. I've seen and done plenty of things in my life that would shock good society. If you object to me, I'll understand, but I've nothing to hide. I kissed Mr. Carson, and I…fancied him something awful. He's a fine man. He wouldn't offer for me." I shrugged, feeling as if I had just ruined my chances. "I didn't want to end up like my ma. I want a better life. I want to mean something to someone. I want a house and children and—"

He had placed his hand over mine. "It's all right." He smiled slightly. "I'm sorry. Now that we've gotten the preliminaries out of the way, perhaps we can go on with our evening and discuss other things."

"I would like that."

"You look like you're about to cry."

"It's been a…confusing time, sir. I'm…a bit out of sorts."

"I'm sorry I upset you." He wasn't as stern now, his gaze softening, lingering on my face. "You're astonishingly beautiful, Eugenia."

"Th-thank you, sir." I hadn't been expecting that compliment.

"I'd like to hear more about your riding and shooting efforts. I was told you wore denim trousers. Is this true?"

"It is. I prefer it to dresses, actually." The weight of the conversation shifted, as the seriousness dissipated. I had spoken my mind on every subject, and he continued to listen attentively. "I'd give anything to burn this corset."

His smile developed into a broad grin, and then he laughed, "I'd pay good money to see that."

Sixteen

By the time I had arrived at the Drover's Cottage, I was a glutton for punishment, and that was exactly what I was going to get. I had heard that Miss Madsen had taken a room at the hotel and that she had met Mr. Hardin. I should have boarded the train to Topeka and left town. I had planned on an evening departure, nearly buying a ticket, but curiosity and a morbid desire to punish myself had brought me out of the saloon, where Marty and I had taken up residence for most of the afternoon, along with several of my junior cowboys.

With a belly full of whiskey, I had sauntered into the hotel that evening, not quite knowing why, but it didn't seem to matter. I was given a table in the dining room, where I found myself hidden behind an enormous fern, watching Eugenia and

Mr. Hardin in discussion. She looked prettier than I could remember, all cleaned up and sporting freshly laundered duds. I had witnessed her arrival, as she had strolled through the room, men's heads turning to watch her. After Mr. Hardin's laughter rang out, an intense burst of jealousy had soured my belly. Eugenia had a certain way about her. She could charm a schoolmarm into not assigning homework for the weekend. I had seen her work her magic on Marty, who had never traveled with anyone, least of all a woman, but that man had come to adore Eugenia.

Before the waitress could arrive at the table, I was on my feet, stalking towards the doors, like a leopard wanting out of captivity. I had seen enough, and I did not need to stay a minute longer. I would retrieve my things and race to the station, hoping to catch the last train out of town. I needed to get as far away from Eugenia as possible. She was in good hands, and I trusted that Mr. Hardin would do right by her. I would go insane if I stayed in Abilene, knowing that she was near or seeing her whenever I came to town. My next job wasn't for another two weeks, and I planned on going home—a rare Wyatt sighting would shock my family.

I had arrived at the station in the nick of time, purchasing a ticket to Topeka. As the train left the station, thundering down the track in the dark of night, I folded a coat and placed it between my head and the window and slept. By the time I emerged from the fog and grogginess of sleep, we were near our destination, the streaks of dawn glinting in the distance. I was eager to disembark, finding the city nearly unchanged since the last time I had been through these parts. I would rent a horse at the stables for the two-hour ride to the Carson Ranch. My kin had not seen me in years, and I was suddenly eager to be surrounded by those I loved and trusted.

For the past decade, I had done nearly everything in my power to avoid this reunion, preferring to mind my own business and finding work in other parts of Kansas and Oklahoma, but now, all I could think about was my mother's home cooking and a friendly face. I spurred the horse on, eager to be home, inhaling the familiar fragrance that was unique to this part of the world: verbena, clover, and thistle. I had helped my pa find this land, when we had arrived from the east, choosing hundreds of acres outside of the town of Elm Hill. I had spent my youth here, learning to ride and shoot and raising hell in town, all before the war. Those years held a special place in my heart, but then pa had been killed in a skirmish with some Missourians and then Bronson and I had left to fight for the Union. Innocence had turned to cold cynicism and dissatisfaction.

I noticed the changes before I reached the house. New fields of corn and wheat spanned out for miles on either side of the road. The farm had been expanded, not just in crops, but buildings. There were three houses; the smallest of which was the original with clapboard siding and a lengthy front porch. There were hired hands about, as well as animals; two dogs ambled over towards me. One was Charlie's pet, Shindy. The other looked like a fluffy mutt.

"Well, I'll be darned," said a familiar voice. I turned to find Bronson, who stood with his hands on his hips. "I never thought I'd live to see the day."

I was going to free the horse from its saddle, but a man came out. "I'll take care of that, sir."

"This is Cutter. He's new."

"Thank you." I untied a bag, dropping it to the ground.

Bronson hugged me, grasping me tightly, which was unexpected. "I'm glad to see you again, brother."

"I heard you ran into some trouble a while back."

He laughed, "When am I not in trouble?"

We began to walk towards the house. "This place has grown."

"We've been busy. I can't wait for you to meet my wife. I have a baby now. Her name is Anna."

Charlie appeared on the front stoop of a nearby house. "I don't believe it!" He held a toddler in his arms. A woman moved behind him. He gave the child to her. "I gotta see my brother." He raced down the steps towards us.

I found myself embraced again, while the strangest sense of gladness crept over me, my eyes shimmering with wetness. The reception was joyous, yet undeserved. I had abandoned my family for years. I did not expect them to welcome me in such a manner. A female shout echoed. It was my mother.

"Wyatt!"

The dogs at my feet picked up on the excitement, their tails wagging enthusiastically, while tongues hung from their mouths. They sniffed my legs repeatedly. A little boy ran out from the third house, followed by another woman. I assumed this was Bronson's wife, Charlotte.

Tears were in my mother's eyes, as she approached. "Oh, my goodness! I knew you'd come home. I knew it!" She flung herself into my arms, and I held her close.

"I really don't deserve this." It was mortifying, but tears fell down my cheeks. This had to stop.

"Oh, Wyatt," she breathed. "We wondered where you were. I've been prayin' for your return. Are you back for good? Are you married?"

Charlie laughed, "He'd never settle, ma. You

know that. Wyatt's all about open spaces and no fences. Isn't that right?"

"That's certainly true." Eugenia's face swam before my mind, and I willed the image to go away.

"Where have you been? You need a bath, son."

"I've come from Abilene. I've been workin' cattle drives." This announcement stunned my brothers. "I know you boys were thinkin' I was still robbin' and swindlin' folks, but I've changed my ways."

Ma grinned. "I knew you'd come around to the right side of the law. Your brother," she glanced at Bronson, "robbed a train last year. He nearly got himself hung for it too. You've yet to hear all the drama. You've missed so much. I now have three beautiful grandbabies." She ruffled the little boy's hair. "This is Dudley. He's Charlotte's son from a previous marriage."

I grinned at the youngster, who was as cute as a button. "How are you?"

"I'm good, sir."

"Charlie and Bronson are livin' here now. They built houses not that long ago. The farm is profitable, and we've a thousand head of cattle. If only Grant would leave that horrible woman he's been seein', everything would be perfect."

Charlie and Bronson's wives had joined us, each woman holding a child. I was introduced, and it was mildly shocking when a baby came my way, as Bronson had handed me his. I had never held an infant in my life, and it felt awkward, especially the way it stared at me, seemingly mesmerized by my face. We had congregated in the house, sitting in the kitchen, while ma began to make a meal, producing several pots and pans. I sat next to Bronson, while the baby was on my lap, playing with the buttons on my shirt. The scene of domestic tranquility was oddly comforting, yet surreal. The women were handsome and congenial, the little boy, Dudley, was charming, and the dogs were underfoot, licking my boots and brushing up against my legs.

By the time supper was ready, I excused myself, needing to use the privy, but I stood outside, staring at the expanse of farmland instead. The aroma of fertile earth with a hint of skunk filled my lungs. The wheat shifted in the breeze, while crickets resonated. It was a moment of reflection and peace—something I didn't even know I needed, but I welcomed it nonetheless. I had wanted to be alone to gather myself, as my family had been overwhelming.

Bronson appeared suddenly, striding around the back of the house. "You okay, Wyatt? You seem out of sorts."

"I…just need a moment."

"Charlie's opened a whiskey bottle."

"Thank the good Lord."

He laughed, "You look well, considering you smell so bad."

I scratched the back of my neck. "I guess that explains how I had the seat to myself on the train."

"You plan on stayin' with us for a spell or are you off again?"

I had not been home more than two hours, and it had affected me in strange and unpredictable ways. It was hard to imagine Bronson having settled so happily, but just looking at him and watching him with his wife told me that he had found exactly what he needed. He adored his children, the baby and the little boy.

"I don't know what my plans are. I just…needed to be here." I headed for the privy. "I can't wait to eat. I'm starvin'."

"We'll be waitin' for you."

The scene at dinner was jovial and familiar, although I was more relaxed than I could remember. The food was excellent. There was apple cider and ice tea, along with brown gravy and roasted chicken. Ma had thrown together a baked apple pudding as well. Charlotte and Rebecca were kind and polite, and it was clear they were close friends. It was after the meal, when I was able to sit with my brothers on the front porch, that the effects of the whiskey had loosened me up— probably too much.

"So, you're a bonafide outlaw, eh, Bronson? I

read about that train robbery in the paper. I wondered if that was you." We rocked back and forth in creaky chairs.

"That was my last job. I paid off the Farley brothers, and we went our separate ways. I donated the rest of the money to the church." He chuckled, "They were quite surprised by that."

"I bet."

"What will you do now?" asked Charlie. "You should stay with us. We can build another house. We've gotten pretty good at it. You should settle and marry. I haven't told anyone, but Rebecca's with child again."

Bronson slapped his knee. "I knew it!"

"You boys are a disgrace," I said in jest. "If I want a hog-killin' time, I'm gonna have to go to town and find Grant. You're both outta commission on that score. I've never seen men more domesticated."

"Ma's makin' plans for a mail order bride again," said Charlie. "We're watchin' all her letters very carefully. I told Rebecca to burn anything that sounds like she's feeding lies to some poor woman."

Eugenia had said she had taken Sofia's place, and Sofia had been corresponding with Mr. Hardin. He was looking for a mail order bride. How long would it be before she married him?

"What's on your mind, Wyatt?" asked

Bronson. "I know that look. You lost somethin'?"

"Maybe I did." I glanced at Charlie, noting his curious expression. "What? Can't a man come home every once in a while?"

"Somethin's troubling you," said Bronson. "It's just us here. Everybody else is inside. I confessed about the train robbery. Maybe you've got somethin' you need to get off your chest."

"He looks love sick."

I glared at Charlie, as anger flared. "The heck you say! What in blazes do you know about that? I'd never shackle myself like you fellas. I look around, and all I see are animals and babies. It's a blasted zoo."

I got to my feet, feeling irritation and restlessness, driving fingers through my hair roughly. I wanted the comfort of my family, but the reunion had been too much. They were all too happy, too content. The women were comely and sweet, the babies adorable, and my brothers beamed from ear to ear, their happiness evident. How could a depressive by nature handle such an onslaught? It was almost too much to bear.

I stalked into the house without another word and hid in a bedroom until everyone had gone. Ma had graciously offered to put on hot water, bringing in a metal tub, which I helped carry. It was comforting—soothing, having my mother attending to my needs, scrubbing my hair with soap and rinsing, while making small talk. She was entirely too pleased that I had returned. When she had finished, she sat in a chair staring at me, while I scrubbed several weeks worth of dirt from my skin.

"You're more than welcome to stay here, Wyatt. I'd be pleased as punch if you did."

I had finished rinsing, sitting back in the tub, while staring at her. "You've done a fine job with the farm. I haven't looked at the books, but I gather you're making a nice pile of money."

"We are."

"Pa would be proud of you."

"I know he would. I'm doin' it all for him."

The house was quiet, only the sound of the clock in the parlor chimed every fifteen minutes. "I didn't mention this to Charlie or Bronson, but…I think I made a mistake."

"What did you do now?"

"I didn't do anything, but I think…I was stupid. I met a woman on the cattle drive. Her name's Eugenia Madsen and…" I could not believe I was about to confess this, "but…I love her."

She smiled, the edges of her eyes crinkling deeply. "Well, well."

"Don't go sendin' out the announcements just yet. Here comes the stupid part. I left her in Abilene, and she's more than likely marrying someone else as we speak."

The smile fell. "What are you sayin'? If you love that woman, you should go get her, son. I didn't raise my boys to be simpletons. Y'all might be the biggest pack of outlaws I ever laid my eyes on, but you were never daft."

"I know."

"If you love her, go back for her." Her grin was broad. "I've got enough room in my heart for more grandbabies."

Her words resonated, penetrating my thick skull. I knew what I had to do. "When's the mornin' train?"

"I've no clue, honey, but I hope you're on it. Bring that woman home. This is where she belongs."

Seventeen

Two days later…

I had a decision to make, and it would not be easy. Mr. Hardin was graciously paying for my stay at the Drover's Cottage, but I felt awkward about accepting his charity, as I was certain I would not marry him. This placed me in a rather dire predicament. I had been restless and agitated, worried over what I would do for a living now, because I would not have the protection of a husband.

The little money in my possession was from Sofia, and, although Mr. Hardin had opened an account for me at the mercantile, I refused to purchase anything on it, preferring to use my own money. I bought a new bonnet and gloves, along with a pair of stockings, but the dresses were old, although I'd had them laundered. The feelings I had for Isaac were the same I would have for a friend, but I suspected he wanted more from me, yet I was in no position to take things further. My thoughts were a jumbled mess, mostly centering on Wyatt, wondering where he had gone and if he would ever return.

I had been invited to dinner last night at the Hardin Ranch, where we had dined on different cuts of beef with biscuits and gravy. The guests had included someone by the name of Bill Hickok, who was the marshal of Abilene and a flamboyant character. Joseph McCoy was the owner of the hotel and stockyards. There were others in attendance that held high positions in business and government. I had felt entirely out of place, wearing the nicest dress I owned, and yet, their wives outshone me in silks and satins, with expertly done hair. Big houses and pretty things were a poor substitute for what I really wanted—Wyatt.

It would be impossible for me to continue on at the hotel, and, with this in mind, I had gathered several notices of employment, which might lead to job opportunities. One was at a school, the other at a small shop on Cedar Street. The hotel was one of the largest buildings in town, and I had discovered it was the headquarters for the Great Western stockyards. Mr. Hardin spent most of his day here, and I would see him frequently as I came and went about my business.

Having lived in the heart of San Antonio all of my life, I had seen many examples of the excesses of men and their drunken behavior, but nothing could possibly compare to the wildness of Abilene, which was the result of the sheer volume of cowboys, who frequented the dance halls, brothels, and The Alamo Saloon. I would never set foot in this part of town at night, and it was risky even in the day, but I needed a job. I had dressed in a functional calico, with a fitted bodice and matching bonnet, while my gloved hands held a drawstring purse.

The lobby teamed with businessmen, all of whom were involved in the cattle trade. I hurried past them, intent on the task at hand, which was the search for employment. An unpleasant thought centered in my gut, an inner knowing of the limits of the choices available and how most of the women in town were engaged in prostitution. It boded ill for me, as I refused to entertain the notion of such work. Perhaps, the idea of marrying Mr. Hardin would appeal to me greater after this day? I hoped not, but I had my doubts.

I left the building, standing on the broad veranda at the front, staring at the carriages, horses, and wagons that ambled by. Several ladies were on the arms of cowboys, and they were dressed provocatively. Eyes were on me; I apprehended their interest, but it was obvious by my clothing and demeanor that I was not one of the "soiled doves", nor would I be, if I had anything to say about it. I was about to step down, when my attention settled upon a man standing to my right. He leaned against the railing with a wide-brimmed hat shading his face, but I knew him in an instant. Stunned, I had not expected to see Wyatt again, ever, but here he stood in the flesh.

"Mr. Carson."

His gaze skimmed over me in a leisurely manner. "I thought I might find you here. You clean up real nice."

"Th-thank you." Flustered and confused, I could hardly contain the violent beating of my heart. "H-how are you?"

"I'm as good as can be expected, darlin'. I'm not in jail or dead."

"You set impossibly low standards for yourself, Mr. Carson."

An eyebrow had risen. "True."

"Are you here on cattle business?"

"Nope."

I dared not hope that he had come for me. "Why are you here then?"

He pushed himself from the wooden beam, stepping closer. "Did you marry him?"

"I beg your pardon?"

"Mr. Hardin." His look had grown stern, the lazy smile disappearing. It was clear it had all been an act.

Before I was able to say another word, he grabbed my hand. "Sir!" Pulling the glove free, he stared at my fingers.

"No ring."

"Of course there isn't a ring!" Indignation rushed through me. "I'm not married, and it's none of your business. Why you should even care is beyond me."

Something changed in his expression, the tension having dissolved, while a certain light gleamed in his eyes. He grabbed me then, hauling me to him, while his lips met mine. I was so utterly unprepared for this that I gasped, while trying to breathe, my heart pounding wildly. The romance of the moment wasn't lost on me, the fragrance of him filling my lungs, while I succumbed to the kiss, returning it eagerly. I was sure we had attracted quite a bit of attention, but it did not matter.

"Grab your things," he said huskily. "We're leavin'."

"W-what?"

"You're comin' with me, but I gotta find a church first."

"What are you saying?"

"I'm marrying you as soon as possible. Then we're goin' home."

It was too much; my poor heart was going to burst. My head began to spin, while I leaned into him for support. "Oh, goodness."

"Will you marry me, Eugenia?"

"I thought you didn't—"

"Forget all of that. I was a fool." He smiled sadly, a look that was laced with regret. "I hope you can forgive me, honey, for being so stupid. I'll spend the rest of my life makin' it up to you. Will you marry me?"

Tears filled my eyes. "I will."

"Then go get your things. We're gettin' married, then we're catchin' a train."

I could hardly believe this turn of events, my body trembling with a combination of feelings, the biggest being shock. He had returned for me. He had offered marriage. I would be with the one I loved…forever.

"I need to leave Mr. Hardin a note. He's been extraordinarily kind to me. I have to thank him."

"You do that." He grinned crookedly. "I'll be waitin'." Before I was able to turn into the hotel, he grabbed me, his hand holding my face, while he kissed me. "I may have lost my mind," he murmured huskily. "But I don't care."

"Oh, Wyatt." He smacked my bottom. "Oh!"

"Get your things. I wanna make the noon train."

I hurried to the room, tossing items into a leather bag, while beaming with happiness. I had never felt this excited about anything in my life. In the lobby, I stopped by reception to write a note to Mr. Hardin, explaining that I was leaving and thanking him for the hospitality. When I left the hotel, Wyatt was waiting, having brought around a carriage. He grinned, while holding open the door.

"My lady."

He helped me alight, while sitting next to me, the driver calling to the horses. "You thought of everything."

Reaching into his pocket, he withdrew something small. "Almost. Give me your hand."

I quickly divested myself of the glove, holding out my hand. He slid a ring upon my finger, a thick gold band. "That's better." It fit perfectly.

"Oh, my stars." I held it up, admiring the gold, which glinted. "Oh, Wyatt." He drew me into his arms, while his lips found mine. "I didn't think you wanted to be shackled with a wife."

"I changed my mind."

"What brought this on?"

"You."

"Where will we live?"

"I'm not sure, but we can stay with my mother for a while. You'll meet my family. There's more babies now than you can shake a stick at."

"I like babies."

His arm was around my shoulders, holding me close. His lips were near my ear. "Then we'll have to get to work on that."

"I can't believe you're here."

"I am, sweetheart. I came back as soon as I could."

He had a haircut and his clothing looked new, even the boots shone with polish. "I would've married you even dirty. It doesn't matter."

"I had to go home. My ma talked some sense into me. She said I was a fool and I should skedaddle on to Abilene and fetch you."

"I think I like her."

"Oh, she's a character, all right. She's happier than I've ever seen her. All her boys will be married and settled now, except for Grant. He's the last hold out." The carriage stopped, the conveyance bouncing. "Looks like we're here." The driver held the door open, lowering the step.

"Can we just do this?" I asked.

"Oh, yeah."

"But…I'm not dressed for church."

"You look fine."

"Who'll be our witness, and isn't there something to sign?"

"It's all taken care of."

He ushered me up the steps, entering a building that smelled of incense and dusty old books. There were people in the front two rows, all of them strangers, men and women and babies. A little blonde boy turned to watch us.

"Who are these people?"

"My family."

Astounded, I stared at him. "What?"

"That's why it took me an extra day to get here." He grinned.

A gray-haired man in a black suit approached. "Good morning," he said, holding out his hand. "I'm Pastor Macmillan. You must be Eugenia Madsen."

"I am." I shook his hand.

"We have a veil for you and some flowers. Then we can begin the ceremony."

"I'm gonna wait for you near the pulpit, all right?" Wyatt's grin was mischievous.

I glanced at the Carsons, who had gathered on my wedding day, having traveled by train to surprise me. I was shocked, nervous, and inundated by waves of happiness so extreme; I thought I might faint. A short, stocky woman approached, her expression courteous, yet determined.

"This must be the lovely Eugenia." She took my hands. "You're a vision to behold, my dear. I'm Mrs. Carson. I'm Wyatt's mother. I want to be the first to welcome you to our family, but we really need to get that veil on you, honey." She glanced at Wyatt. "You go stand over there, and your bride will join you shortly."

"Yes, mother," he chuckled.

"It's g-good to meet you," I said, my voice

quivering. A pretty white lace went over my head, and a bundle of flowers was in my hands. "Oh, my."

Mrs. Carson grinned with smug, yet happy satisfaction. "You're ready now. All you have to do is wait for the music and walk towards Wyatt. Can you do that?"

Tears had fallen, as my throat constricted. "I will, yes." Mrs. Carson left me then, hurrying to take her seat, while I began to cry even harder, thoroughly overcome by emotion. I did not know it would end like this, but I had always held out hope that one day…I would marry the one I loved. That day was at hand.

The End

Epilogue

Are you all right?" We were finally alone, having left the reception twenty minutes ago.

"Yes."

He sat on the bed, loosening his necktie, while I stared in the mirror, not quite believing that I was married. His family had returned to the Carson Ranch, while Wyatt and I would honeymoon at the Drover's Cottage. We would follow in a day or two. Glancing at him through the mirror, I almost could not believe that I was Mrs. Wyatt Carson.

"Come here."

"Did it really happen?"

His smile was endearing. "It did. It's legal and blessed in the eyes of the church and my family, of course."

"I'm scarcely afraid to admit to being this

happy."

"You can be as happy as you like." He'd pulled his boots off, tossing them aside.

"You were so horrible to me. What was it you said? You didn't want to make me any promises because you were liable to break them." I approached the bed, and he placed his hands on my hips. I ran my fingers through his hair, feeling the silky strands.

"I've never been someone a woman can rely on, honey, but for you, I'm gonna take that chance. When I got on that train to Topeka, I knew I'd made a dreadful mistake. The further I got from you, the worse I felt. My ma set me straight."

"I like your mother…a great deal."

"It seems all her daughters-in-law get on like a house on fire. You'll fit right in."

"Won't they be appalled that I was raised in a brothel?"

"Everybody has a past, darlin'. It's the Wild West. Nobody cares about bloodlines and breeding. As long as you don't fall asleep at the dinner table, you should do fine."

I giggled, "Oh, my." He'd begun to work the buttons on my bodice. "I can't believe we're here."

"Believe it."

The garment loosened. It wasn't dark yet, as sunlight streamed in through the sheer curtains. "Shouldn't we close the drapes?"

"Are you shy?"

"Yes, I am. You might've bedded all of Texas and Kansas, but I've never done this."

His laughter filled the room. "Go close 'em."

I hurried, drawing the drapes shut, plunging the room into darkness, although the lamp gave off a fair amount of light. I stepped out of the petticoats and skirt, leaving the bodice and corset on a chair. The stockings were rolled down my legs, one at a time, and discarded on the floor. I wore a thin chemise and drawers; the latter I stepped out of quickly. He reached a hand to me, and I took it, sitting on the bed.

"You sure are beautiful. That time by the river, when you swam in that shift, I could see everything."

Alarmed, I breathed, "No!"

He nodded. "Yes, ma'am. Those breasts are a work of art."

I had begun to pull the pins from my hair, while dark tresses tumbled to my shoulders and beyond. "I didn't know that."

"I thought you were a tease."

"I...guess. Where you're concerned."

"What about Scott? You can't say you weren't taken by that handsome cowboy."

"He was fine, but I always preferred you," I giggled. I marveled at how easy it was to be with him, to talk to him, and how I yearned to feel his nakedness against mine. He had begun to remove his pants, kicking the trousers off. His underthings were the only article of clothing left on his body. "You look very nice."

"Yeah?"

I admired his chest, the muscles sculpted and protruding, topped off with tiny nipples, while his belly was taut and smattered with hair. He had bathed and shaved recently; his smell was slightly musky, with hints of whatever soap he had used. Feeling bold and adventurous, I sat on him, gazing down at his handsome face, which was fixated on me.

"What would you have done, if I had married Mr. Hardin? I was dangerously close to considering it, Wyatt. I was nearly out of options."

"Thank God I wasn't any later."

"I'm glad I didn't act impulsively. I sometimes jump in without thinking."

"Like today?"

"Yes." I leaned over him, my hair falling onto his chest. "I took a chance today. I might regret it for the rest of my life, but I don't care. I love you, Wyatt Carson."

"Here I was, enjoying the open road, seeking my fill of whiskey and women whenever and wherever I saw fit, and then you came along to spoil it all. You've ruined me for all other women."

"Truly? From what I've seen of men, most are

hardly faithful, and the rest indifferent."

"I don't plan on cheatin' or neglecting you, darlin'. I'm gonna be hands on from this day forward." He grinned crookedly.

He grasped the chemise, lifting it over my head. My hair fell over my chest, as a small measure of protection, but from the heated look in his eye, he would see and touch every inch of me. I shivered in anticipation, my belly trembling with pinpricks of pleasure. I had plans for him as well, because his anatomy felt quite agitated, twitching and growing harder beneath me by the second. I would explore him...thoroughly.

He sat up suddenly, his arms enfolding me, while his lips captured mine for a long, languid kiss. When he released me, he whispered, "Lord I love you, woman. You drive me crazy. To think that you're mine now, lock, stock, and barrel, I still can't believe it."

I placed my finger on his mouth. "Don't talk, Wyatt. Just love me."

"Yes, ma'am."

Preview of
A Mail Order Bride For Grant

The Carson Brothers of Kansas
Book Four

Sleep wasn't a half bad idea. I took my own room, which was down the hall from the lovely Caldwell sister's. I tossed my boots in the corner, leaving my hat and holster on the table and crawled into bed, exhaustion claiming me almost instantly. By the time I woke, I was ready for the washroom, wanting to cleanse away all traces of the night I had spent in jail.

By six sharp, I was ready to meet the ladies, waiting for them in the reception area, while people came and went. An evening train had arrived and travelers wanted accommodations. After twenty minutes, I began to worry that Eva had changed her mind. I was about to go up, when the younger one, Cora appeared.

"Hello, Mr. Carson." She smiled prettily.

"Good evenin'."

"My sister's on her way. I'm sorry we're late."

"It's all right."

She looked similar to her sister, the blonde hair, the blue eyes, but her face was thinner. Her traveling dress was a peach concoction with a high neckline. A black shawl was draped around her shoulders. Movement caught my attention, as I spied Eva. She had taken the time to do her hair, while her frilly white dress was bustled at the back with a square décolletage. I'd only seen her in the day dress, which had not revealed any skin. What greeted me now was an impossibly beautiful woman, whose decidedly feminine shape had been molded to perfection, the tops of her breasts like the crown jewels in a king's coronet. The only thing lacking was a smile, as she scowled at me.

"Evenin', Miss Caldwell." I took her gloved hand, kissing it. "You look lovely." I watched her carefully, noting that she swallowed visibly.

"T-thank you."

"Is everything all right? You seem unhappy about something."

"I…just…you don't have to do this."

"Do what?"

"Dinner. We're perfectly capable of feeding ourselves."

"But then I would've missed seeing you looking so…" my gaze skimmed over the fullness of her cleavage, "delectable."

She slid her hand free, her lips pursed. "Let's just eat, so we can get this over with."

I'd learned a thing or two about females over the course of my life, and although she feigned indifference, even hostility towards me, I knew she was any but indifferent. Not only had she taken the time—careful time to arrange herself this evening, but I detected the hint of rose cologne. On her it was like a spring bouquet, the aroma melded perfectly with the sweetness of her skin creating an intoxicating scent. It seemed I hadn't been the only one to visit the washroom today.

"I'm starved," said Cora. "I hope they serve custard and stewed fruit. If I could, I'd eat dessert first."

"I'm sure you would." I escorted the ladies into the dining room, which was filled with men and women, who sat amidst tables covered in lace cloths and candles. "I've reserved a table." Several heads turned in our direction. I held out the chair for Eva. "Here you are."

"Thank you."

I did the same for Cora, who smiled brightly. "Thank you, Mr. Carson."

"You can call me Grant. We needn't be so formal." I took my seat, while a waiter came over.

"Good evening," he said. "What refreshments would you ladies like?"

"Wine would be wonderful," said Cora.

"And she'll have the lemonade. I'll have a glass of wine." Eva gave her sister a look.

Cora pouted. "That's not fair at all."

"And you sir?"

"Whiskey."

"The special is roast veal with vegetables. We're offering plum pudding and cheesecake for dessert."

"That sounds marvelous," gushed Cora. "I love plum pudding."

Once we had decided on our meals, the waiter returned with the drinks, Eva sipping her glass of wine delicately. I was fascinated by the way the candlelight lit her face, the angles of her cheekbones and the fullness of her mouth were…distracting. I could stare at her indefinitely, which was slightly worrying.

I had not encountered another woman since May, who had captured my attention like this. While the conversation centered on small talk, I was busy formulating and discarding several schemes, as to how I could continue to see Eva. I had to know what she intended, but her answers were cagey. The furtive look in her eye was evidence that she was hiding something. This trip to Kansas was far more complicated and deliberate then she would dare admit.

"So, Mr. Carson—Grant. What do you do, sir?"

I glanced at Cora. "I'm into a bit of everything."

"That's so vague."

"I've rustled cattle. I've worked on the family farm. I've done the odd job here and there."

"You're a jack of all trades," murmured Eva.

"It seems that way." I sat back in the chair. "What brings you to Kansas?"

"A change of scenery," said Eva.

I didn't believe that for one minute. "Uh-huh. Will you be settling in Topeka?"

"I'm not certain. We might or we might not."

"It all depends on where we open our business—ouch!" Cora glared at Eva. There had been movement under the table; someone had been kicked.

"Business?" Now this had my attention. "What sort of business?"

"Nothing you need to concern yourself with, Mr. Carson." Eva took a sip of wine.

Cora scowled. "How are we supposed to have a conversation when you won't let me talk?"

"He needn't know about our plans, darling." There was an edge of warning in her tone. "He's a stranger, remember? What do we do with strangers?"

"We…avoid them?"

She nodded. "Yes."

"But he helped you, Eva. He sprung you from jail. You're always doing things you shouldn't and he was kind enough to help."

"Everything I've done is for our welfare, for *your* welfare. But, I don't wish to talk about that."

"Your penchant for robbing men?" I grinned at her expression. She looked like she wanted to murder me. "Remind me not to sit next to you on a train."

The arrival of our food halted the conversation, which was a shame. We ate in silence, while I continued to stare at Eva, marveling at the way she delicately cut her beef and chewed the tiny pieces. The less she said about herself, the more I wanted to know. I'd met women who were practiced at artifice, purposely creating an aura of mystery, but Eva was the real deal. She was a woman on a mission, and I would find out what it was.

After we had eaten, I escorted the ladies to their room, although Eva had objected rather strenuously. Cora had disappeared inside, while I stood by the door with her sister.

"I'm not the enemy, you know."

"I didn't think you were."

She was so stiff, so in control. I longed to shake her, to snap her out of this posture. "Are you staying in Topeka?"

"Maybe. I'm not certain…yet."

"What are you here for?"

"That's really none of your business. I appreciate everything you've done for me, I truly do, but we needn't continue this. I'm quite happy to manage everything from here on out. I'm very good at taking care of myself."

"Where are you from? Where is your family?"

"I'm from Ohio. I don't have family. Cora and I are orphans."

I hadn't known that, but I might have guessed. "I'm sorry."

"It's nothing for you to be sorry about."

"I would like to help you ladies, but I first need to know what you're about."

Her look was smug. "Well, that won't be possible. We're on our way tomorrow." She held out her hand. "Thank you for all your help. You've been one of the kindest men I've ever met. I do mean that. I'm sure if things were different…perhaps…oh, never mind."

I was not content with her hand, pulling her to me. She stiffened in my arms, but then relaxed, as I inhaled the aroma of her scent. I had closed my eyes, savoring the feeling of her in my arms. She pushed me away a moment later.

"Good evening, Mr. Carson."

"Grant."

"Goodbye, Grant." She opened the door, closing it behind her.

I stood in the hallway staring at the door, filled with the oddest sense of regret. It was like reading a novel, where the book ended midway without a proper conclusion. This could not possibly be the end for us. It felt more like a beginning, but this woman was determined to give me a run for my money. I had every intention of finding out what her plans were. I would not be so easily dissuaded.

Returning to my room, I began to remove my coat, draping it over a chair, while unbuttoning my vest. Reaching into a pocket, I had meant to retrieve the billfold, but I couldn't find it. I drove my hand into my pants, looking for it. In that shocking, disquieting moment, it became clear that Miss Caldwell had robbed me. I had graciously rescued her from jail, fed her twice today, taken her to Topeka, and she had robbed me! Anger, the likes of which I rarely felt, surged through me, producing steam that exploded from my ears.

I left the room, stomping my way down the corridor, while a white-hot anger had me pounding on the door. "Open up, you little tart! You stole my billfold!" I tried the knob, but it would not turn. I slammed my fists against the wood, the sound echoing in the hallway. "Open this door!"

Cora appeared before me. "What is it?"

"I told you not to open the door!" Eva had

undressed, wearing only a chemise and drawers. She held a blanket to her chest. "Don't let him in!"

I stormed into the room. "After everything I've done for you, you'd rob me?"

"Is this true, Eva? Did you steal his money?" She glared at her sister.

"I…I…didn't mean to."

"Oh, Eva! How could you? I can't believe it."

"Why you little—" I had wanted to help this woman, knowing that she was in over her head and all alone. But she had driven these emotions from me, leaving me entirely enraged. I grasped her by the shoulders, shaking her. "I ought to throttle you!"

"I really didn't mean it. My fingers have a way of…betraying me. I'm sorry!"

"That's not good enough!" I tossed her to the bed, landing on top of her, while she squirmed beneath me.

"Sir!"

Cora stood by the window watching. "What are you doing, Mr. Carson? If you harm one hair on her head, I'll hit you with this chair."

"I'm not gonna hurt her. Hold still, you little wench!" I grasped her hands, bringing them over her head. "I got a few things to say to you, but first, I think I'm owed a kiss. That's the smallest amount of payment for the trouble you've caused me."

"Go to hell!" She would not hold still, turning her head from side to side, while a deep flush had appeared on her chest.

"Maybe this will teach her a lesson," murmured Cora. "She's gotta stop robbing men. It's caused nothin' but trouble since we left Ohio. Kansas men are smarter, Eva. You gotta watch yourself. You're getting everything you deserve, by the way."

"Hit him with the chair!"

"Where's his billfold? I'll give him his money and he'll be on his way, although it's a shame."

"I'll get my money, but first…" I had pressed myself into her, feeling every curve of her body, which had been a mistake. I was going to kiss the little vixen, but I knew it would take a near Herculean effort to drag myself away. "You've got this comin', and you know it." I'd grasped her head, holding her in place, while she gazed at me with startled eyes. "Lord, you're a handsome woman. Irritating, but handsome."

Our lips met, while she tried to turn from me, but I was determined, closing my mouth over hers. She gasped, trembling beneath me, as I slid my tongue between her lips. I thought she would continue to struggle, but she had gone slack, giving me the upper hand. She tasted of wine and pudding, a sweetly delicious combination. I had opened my eyes to stare at her, observing hers were closed. The kiss was relentless, soft, yet deeply stirring, hardening certain parts of my anatomy to distracting proportions. Tiny, breathy mewls left her throat, while her fingers threaded through my hair.

She was mine now.

"I think that's quite enough, Mr. Carson."

I had forgotten about Cora. Tearing myself away from Eva's eager mouth, I gazed upon her, seeing a woman who had succumbed to me rather easily. She knew it too, her look hardening.

"Get out!"

It was disappointing knowing that I could not trust her, although I wanted to. She did not want my help, although she desired me. I knew that much. I left the bed, adjusting my pants. "I guess I'll take my billfold then."

"Here you are. I'm sorry about that, sir. I don't know why she took your money. We have plenty of our own."

Eva had lifted herself onto her elbows, staring at me, while relief and confusion graced her comely features. "I…am sorry."

"Well, that's just rich." I sounded bitter. "I've met your kind before, honey. You're all take and no give, but that kiss was nice. That was the least you could do for me, although…" I grinned crookedly, "maybe you'd like to come to my room. If it's money you're after, I'd pay top dollar for a night. You seem willin' enough."

She scrambled from the bed, reaching into a drawer. "Get out!" A shiny knife was in her hand, glinting by lamplight. "You go now! I'm sorry about it all, but that's enough."

I nodded. "Predictable. You sure showed your true colors, eh? I should've known the innocent get up was all an act. Darn, but you sure had me fooled." I strode towards the door. "You ladies have a nice life now. I wish you good luck on your journeys." I slammed it behind me, as I stalked down the hallway. I had enjoyed every second of that kiss and then some, but a woman like that could ruin a man.

Manufactured by Amazon.ca
Bolton, ON

35546218R00109